X

The Music of
Summer

The Music of Summer

Rosa Guy

F
Guy

Published by
Delacorte Press
Bantam Doubleday Dell Publishing Group, Inc.
1540 Broadway
New York, New York 10036

Library of Congress Cataloging-in-Publication Data

Guy, Rosa
The music of summer / Rosa Guy.
p.   cm.
Summary: The attractive, sophisticated young African-Americans
gathered at Cape Cod have their own set of economic color prejudices;
but Sarah, the darkest-skinned, begins to see more clearly the duties
and hope of her ancestry.
ISBN 0-385-30599-0
[1. Afro-Americans—Fiction.]   I. Title.
PZ7.G987Mu   1992
[Fic]—dc20   91-22464
                                                     CIP
                                                     AC

Book design by Christine Swirnoff
Manufactured in the United States of America

March 1992

10 9 8 7 6 5 4 3 2

BVG

Dedicated to the Guys

Warner Guy III,
Warner Guy IV,
Charles Guy,
Otonia Guy,
and Ameze Rosa Guy—
my grandchildren

The Music of Summer

One

 "Sarah Richardson! Where do you think you're going?" Sarah's heart leapt, then pounded against her chest. Closing the door, she looked up the hallway. Her mother, with her hands on her hips, stood outside the kitchen. The sunlight from the living room framed her.

"I—I—I . . ." Sarah wanted to lie. Habit prevented her. She had never lied to her mother. Why hadn't she gone out before Lottie came in from work? She had intended to. Sneaking out with her mother in the house made no sense.

Sarah sighed. "I—I'm running over to Cathy's for—"

"No! You don't mean that! You can't mean you're going over to that woman's house without telling me!"

"Ma, I'm going to see Cathy—not her mother. I'll only be a few minutes."

"Then make her come here! That Cathy Johnson didn't

mind making a nuisance of herself when she needed your help. Since she passed, not once has she rung this bell. That's the thanks I get for tolerating her and her snooty friends around my living room while you tried to push sense into Cathy's twisted little brain. The same thing happened when you helped her out with her college entrance exams. That li'l hussy's worse than her mother!"

Sarah bowed her head, trying to think up a reason to give her mother. One that she would accept. How could she give the real reason? Impossible. "I—I'm going to pick up something I left over there the last time I went," Sarah said. She did have a sweater that she might need over at Cathy's.

"If it stayed there this long, it can't be important," her mother said. "Call her. Make her bring it. Or better yet, ask her to leave it with the doorman."

"She's busy, Ma. She and Mrs. Johnson will be rushing around shopping. It's almost time for them to be leaving for the Cape."

"I don't give one good damn how busy that li'l leech is. She owes you. Who else could she get to give as much time to her as you? Forsaking your schoolwork, your music—like you're her goddamn slave.

"I raised you to be proud, Sarah Richardson, to walk with your head held high. I can't stand thinking of you going around sniffing other folks' tails—begging. . . ."

"Mother—you and Mrs. Johnson were such good friends. She's still your friend—the best you ever had." Sarah and her mother were alike in one way. They didn't make friends easily. Since Lottie and Clarice had broken off their friendship, no other woman had taken Mrs. Johnson's place.

Now it seemed that she and Cathy were on the verge of an irreparable break—through no fault of hers. Oh, God, she hated the thought! Who in this life could take Cathy's place?

"Sarah Richardson, don't you be telling me who my friends are. I spent a long time finding out about the likes of the Clarice Johnsons of the world. A lifetime! I know what makes a friend a friend. I know who mine are—and yours too."

Sarah bit her full bottom lip. If she said one more word, Lottie would try to stop her going. Or at the very least demand to know her real reason for going. How could she explain that she wanted to ask Cathy face to face why she hadn't been invited to her upcoming tea? A tea! She thought of thunder, of lightning. Thunder in her mother's voice, lightning in her eyes.

Who but Cathy Johnson had the audacity to change evening get-togethers into afternoon teas and have everyone clamoring to attend? Sarah had always admired that in Cathy—her audacity. That's what had kept them together through the years—their differences. It had made their relationship interesting. Sarah followed rules of discipline. Cathy delighted in bending rules to suit herself, and didn't give a damn. Everyone followed her.

Sarah had heard about Cathy's teas that day, from another girl who had not been invited. The girl had heard about it from Fred Hamilton, who had been invited. That made being there doubly important. To be around Fred Hamilton—in the same room with him, to talk to him, watch him talking to others . . .

3

Cathy and Fred were dating. But Cathy went through boy-friends like Kleenex. Sarah wanted to be around when Cathy discarded Fred and he needed support from a friend. She wanted to be that friend.

But what was more important than the tea, more important than Fred, was that Cathy had been acting strangely. Sarah had to know why. It was already the end of June, almost July Fourth, the time when Cathy and Mother bundled off to the Cape. The tea had to be soon. Yet Cathy hadn't called, asking her to the tea.

"Mrs. Johnson's always glad to see me," Sarah said.

"Why shouldn't she be? You took the responsibility of that empty-headed daughter off her hands. If not for you Cathy'd still be in first grade."

"She always asks for you," Sarah kept on, determined to support Mrs. Johnson in what she considered a senseless quarrel. "She said she's called here dozens of times."

"Tell Clarice Johnson to keep her calls," Lottie snapped. "If she wants to see me, she knows where this house is. This building hasn't gone nowhere since she moved out."

"Ma, I swear I'll dash there and back. I have to see Cathy. It's real important. Whatever you think, Cathy's still my best friend."

"No, she ain't, Sarah. I'm your best friend. Me! And your aunt Gladys and uncle Sam. Don't go letting those don't-give-a-damn high-yeller folks control the lever of your life!"

"I know! I know! I know you are my best friends," Sarah shouted, losing control.

Startled, her mother searched Sarah's eyes. Then she let her gaze move over the tall, slim body in its jeans and

T-shirt. When she saw the clenched fists, Lottie closed her face, tightened it, and went into the kitchen. Sarah waited at the door in the silence. She waited to hear the loud voice, with its rage, yelling from the kitchen. Instead there was only silence. That silence unnerved her. She had never before raised her voice to her mother. Had it really been that easy to quiet her? Not that she would do it again. Never did she want to have quarreling become a way of life the way it had between Cathy and Mrs. Johnson. Still, Lottie had to understand that she was seventeen. There were things she had to decide for herself.

Guilt. The silence had given her permission to leave. But how could she just go out and leave her mother simmering in rage? Sarah walked down to the kitchen and stood looking in at her mother, basting a leg of lamb. How could she break the silence without compromising her intentions? For, no matter what Lottie said, she intended to go.

After what might have been an eternity, Lottie finally spoke. "Don't forget this is the night your uncle Sam and aunt Gladys come for dinner. Don't keep us waiting. Your uncle Sam doesn't like reheated food and I can't stand it cold."

"I know. I know." Sarah fought against a resurgence of anger. Uncle Sam and Aunt Gladys came for dinner every Thursday. They came to listen to her play the piano. That had been a ritual for years, part of the master plan of their lives. Only once—and this was what her mother alluded to —had Sarah ever disappointed them. And that time it had been because of Cathy. Always Cathy. But then, Cathy Johnson had been interwoven into her life from early childhood to early teens—until Mrs. Johnson had moved from their Parkview apartment to her Riverview apartment.

She and Cathy had loved each other. They had fought—sometimes with fists, but more often with their eyes. Sarah preferred to fight Cathy with eyes. Cathy was stronger. But Sarah's round, brown smiling eyes were more than a match for Cathy's smoky blue mischievous laughing eyes. One sensed the devil at work in them. They charmed her. Yet Sarah always resisted their charm.

They had been key-around-the-neck kids, their mothers working. Cathy had refused to study after school. She loved the forbidden candy stores where kids smoked and petted. Sometimes she went into the park and came home late. Staring into her eyes, she would say to Sarah, " 'Fraidy-cat, coward," or "When do you show a bit of courage . . ." or "You're an old-fashioned stick-in-the-mud," or "I don't want to be your friend. You're too square. . . ."

Sarah always wanted to be with Cathy. Cathy knew it. But Sarah had a rigid discipline that she refused to break. She practiced, loved music, and feared Lottie.

However, Cathy, a generous girl, never remained angry. The next day she came with ice cream or potato chips, or soda—softening Sarah up for her next attempt at seduction.

On the Thursday Sarah had missed dinner with Uncle Sam and Aunt Gladys, she had gone early to the park with Cathy. They went to the zoo, ate hot dogs and Cracker Jacks, then ice cream. They had flirted with boys. Cathy had stopped to talk to groups of boys whom she knew. But mostly they had walked and talked. Then Cathy, with a mischievous glint in her eyes, had said, "Bet your uncle Sam and your aunt Gladys are gone by now." Sarah had not noticed the time. Cathy had. She had planned it that way. In a panic Sarah had rushed home to meet Uncle Sam and Aunt Gladys at the door leaving.

Uncle Sam hadn't scolded. But the disappointment that shone through his eyes had stirred an agony of guilt that Sarah had never forgotten. Never again had she gone out on Thursday evenings.

"Sure, you're getting to be a big girl now," said Lottie, interrupting Sarah's reflection. Still she refused to look at Sarah. "Nowadays it's hard to say to someone who thinks that she's grown that all she got to think about is hard work and reaching a bunch of goals. But that's what it's all about, Sarah. That's what it's been for me—and that's what it's gonna be for you. We dark-skinned Americans always had to keep our eyes on goals." She slammed the roast back in the oven, then looked at Sarah. "Believe me—what we do, or don't do, depends on us. Life for us is one mighty sea. The waters are damn choppy, so we got to be good swimmers—and that's gospel!"

The kitchen sparkled. Down the hall the living room had been made into a wonderland by sunlight rushing through the windows. Their windows overlooked Central Park. In those Black-Is-Beautiful times of the seventies that Lottie Richardson and Clarice Johnson bragged about, Mrs. Johnson had helped them get into the Parkview apartment.

The women had met while working for the unemployment agency. They did the same work and earned the same salary. Mrs. Johnson had been living in Parkview. Lottie and Sarah had still been living with Uncle Sam. When Lottie had applied for the apartment she had been turned down. Then Mrs. Johnson had convinced the management that she had to have a second apartment. She rented it, then late one night she had helped Lottie to move in.

Management had found out. Lottie was asked to move. Then the real battle, involving the NAACP, had been fought in the courts and Lottie had won. Until then, the occupants of the building had been light-skinned men and women and black men who handled big money.

But much had happened since that time. Lottie had become supervisor of her department. Clarice had found a job in the business she had studied so long and so hard: interior decorating. Things changed, things changed, things changed.

Sarah's gaze settled on her mother's lively dark, dimpled made-for-laughing face. "Gosh, Ma, you're real pretty when you get mad." She waited, knowing there was a struggle going on inside Lottie. Finally Lottie shook her head. The tightened skin about her mouth relaxed, then pulled back to expose pretty white teeth. Her dimples sank deeper. They laughed together. Free of guilt, Sarah walked down the hall and out the door.

In the elevator Sarah kept thinking of her mother's beautiful face. How different she looked now from the pictures of her with which Uncle Sam and Aunt Gladys decorated their walls. In those pictures a young, very skinny, homely Lottie Richardson strained to stare out of their frames. But in recent years plumpness had stretched her into beauty. Weight had given her presence, her job had given her authority. In the photographs taken on Sarah's graduation, May 1984,

Lottie—the smiling woman with her serious-faced, father-less daughter—looked absolutely stunning.

The elevator slid to street level and Sarah walked out into crowds of rowdy children flowing from the lobby to the stoop. Teenagers flirted, giggled, talking loud, while the doorman, having long ago given up on keeping lobby or stoop clear of children, looked over their heads with habitual disdain.

Maneuvering to get out of the building, Sarah nodded to teenagers, most of whom she had known since babyhood. Their rapid growth never ceased to amaze her, particularly the boys—their energy was awesome. One almost smelled their strength. The word testosterone jumped to mind. The girls pushing through to early womanhood. They responded to the boys by putting on thick makeup, big earrings, and looks of wide-eyed admiration.

They had little to say to Sarah, and she had little to say to them. Her seriousness didn't attract the interest of a younger group—no more than it did girls of her own age. She hadn't attended the neighborhood high schools, going instead to the LaGuardia School for Music and Art before graduating to Juilliard.

Sarah walked away from the stoop, hardly hearing the loud chatter, which her mother hated. Lottie wanted to move—particularly since Mrs. Johnson had. It had been three years now. She had searched but had found nothing to compare with their lovely Parkview apartment. Uncle Sam liked to tease: "Lottie," he said, "you living in the last bastion for colored folks. Ain't no more so-called luxury buildings gonna be built for you-all. If they are, it sure ain't gonna be below this park. Y'all stuck. This here park's y'all's buffer zone." Except that Clarice had moved into an apartment overlooking the Hudson River—something Lottie didn't forget or forgive.

Sarah walked into the park. The warm breeze caressed her face, blew into her thick, coarse hair, entered her nostrils, bringing with it the smell of new green. Sarah hugged herself. She loved the park. As she walked the path going west to the opposite exit, the bright green of trees titillated her. The bright blue sky sprinkled with white, white clouds opened a way for her. She moved from herself—a spirit in slow motion, floating through fields of weeds, of flowers, of sunflowers bending to the force of the breeze. Tiny animals scurried beneath her. Languid butterflies fluttered from flower to weed, from weed to flower. The bright flowers of the sun guided her to the distant way where clouds joined, thickened to create a haze, a castle, which the bright beams of the sun touched with gold. An incredible freedom invaded her. She floated up to the gates, her mouth opening wide in laughter exposing Lottie-looking teeth flashing white against her smooth black skin. . . .

Hard concrete hit the soles of her sneakers and jolted Sarah. Honking horns, screeching brakes, and a taxi driver cursing from his window made her jump back to the curb. The traffic light had turned red. Sarah moved her eyes around, averting stares from passersby puzzled by her seemingly pointless laughter. Sarah forced her laughter away— but it faded slowly. She enjoyed those moments stolen from her dreary disciplined life.

Walking on to Riverside Drive, Sarah had turned the corner of Cathy's block when she saw Fred Hamilton leaving her stoop. He walked past without noticing her and she had to call: "Fred?"

"Hey." He stopped and walked back to her. "Whatcha know, Sarah. Why are you so late? Teatime is just about over."

"Oh?" She blanked her face to hide dismay. So the tea, the grand tea to which she hadn't been invited, had happened today. And so had the opportunity to be in the same room with Fred, talk to him, ask him about himself. "How did it go?" she asked.

"What?"

"The tea."

"Okay," he said, shrugging.

"Enjoy yourself?"

He grimaced. "Tea. What's that? I ain't British. Anyway I had to leave. Got to go for practice . . ."

Sarah tried to catch his eyes. He looked away, up the block. "Is Cathy home?" she asked.

"Sure. Folks are still up there—the gang. They making plans for the trip to the Cape. You going?"

Sarah tried to ignore the pain that stabbed at her chest. "Are you?" she asked in turn.

"Guess so. Great to get out of this city for a while. I don't think I can stay the whole summer, though—practice. you know. . . ."

Pain dug deeper. Once upon a time she and the Johnsons had talked about her going to the Cape. In her life there were two issues, always important: her lessons and money.

They had always made it impossible for her to go. In recent years Cathy had not asked.

"I'm sure Cathy'll find a way to make you stay," Sarah said.

"She's got her other friends," Fred said then, with a show of resentment. "Milt James'll be going. Know him?"

"Yes, I know him."

"She'll forget I'm even around," he said.

Sarah didn't believe that. Nevertheless she asked, "So— why are you going at all?"

He glanced at Sarah, then away again. "What can I tell you? I like the girl. Well, I got to go, Sarah, be seeing you— maybe at the Cape?"

Sarah stood watching him until he turned the corner. She wished she hadn't drawn that confession.

She had known Fred Hamilton for a long time. First as a little boy playing basketball in schoolyards. She had been taller than he, and bigger. She had had to defend him from big boys who took things from him. At thirteen he had grown into a tall, lanky boy, still dunking balls into baskets in schoolyards. Now, at nineteen, Fred Hamilton had become handsome, the dream man of girls. Since being offered the chance in the college big leagues, he had become important to Cathy.

What should she do now? The tea had already been. Fred had drunk his and gone. Why bother? There remained the issue of friendship. Why should it be left to Cathy alone to break the ties of so many years? Why shouldn't she have the opportunity to say yes or no—or how dare you. . . .

Two

 Cathy's smoky blue eyes widened when she opened the door and saw Sarah. They stared at each other, Sarah and Cathy, appraising each other. "Sarah," she said finally, "what are you doing here?"

"I—I was passing by," Sarah said, "so I decided to drop in." The lie made it impossible for her to confront Cathy. But seeing Cathy she didn't want to, deciding instead that holding on to their friendship had to be more important.

"Well, you're here now." Cathy spoke airily. She stepped aside. Sarah went in.

She wanted to bolt at her friend's attitude. She wanted to call up the pride that her mother insisted she show. Instead she walked down the long hallway, Cathy behind her.

She and Cathy were the same height—five feet eight, both slim. Cathy had fair skin and honey-blond hair that hung to her shoulders. She wore makeup and knew how to apply colors skillfully to bring out the blue of her eyes. Her outfit for tea was a blue silk blouse over a straight skirt. The tea had been a dressy affair.

Sarah had never worn makeup. Her poreless, smooth black skin and wide, round eyes gave her the look of innocence. Her uncle thought she was beautiful. She saw herself through her uncle's eyes. Beautiful. As she walked down the long hall she had to keep that in mind to make up for feeling out of place in a T-shirt and jeans.

Valerie and Hester, two white girls who lived in the building, came out in the hallway as Sarah neared the living room. "Sorry we have to leave, Cathy," Valerie said, "but we have another date." She saw Sarah and smiled. "Why so late, Sarah? Tea started at two. It's already four."

"Must you go?" Cathy smiled into Valerie's eyes. "We never get a chance to really chat. . . ." This meant that Cathy hadn't been able to seduce her neighbors. She probably hadn't had enough time.

She walked back to the door with them, coaxing, trying to change their minds, while Sarah stood at the living-room door, looking in.

Cathy's three remaining guests were her regulars from Banning High School days. There was Sheila—tall, thin, white skin, with straight black hair, which she wore bobbed twenties style. Sheila's father, a successful business lawyer, had gone to Howard University, where Sheila was now studying law. And there was Betty—her parents were both professors teaching at universities in New Jersey. Of all Cathy's friends Betty acted the most down-to-earth—except

14

for her babyish talk. She had a light golden-brown complexion, golden-brown curly hair, and amber-colored eyes, which gave the impression that she was always laughing inside. Milton James, the only remaining male, was about six nine and thin. The fading adolescent acne that dotted his face resembled freckles. He was a "red"—skin red, kinky reddish hair, and watery blue eyes. Milt's father was a big black ex-boxer who had gone into the real-estate business. He owned real estate in Washington Heights. His mother, a tiny Swiss woman with prematurely gray hair, drove a big Lincoln Continental, conspicuously, from their residence in upstate New York to her husband's agencies, through the inner-city streets.

Mrs. Johnson always said that Milt's father ought to have kept the "poor boy" with the white folks upstate where he had spent his sheltered childhood. Instead his father forced him to visit the inner city. He wanted his son to have a sense of identity—an identity that Milt repudiated. He also wanted Milt to get to know his real-estate business, which he would one day inherit. Mr. James had put him into the Banning private school to get him familiar with interracial harmony. "That," Mrs. Johnson said, "made the boy just one confused sucker."

A surly expression floated over Milt's undefined features, threatening to settle as character. One prayed it wouldn't. Sarah already disliked Milt as it was. She had known him one year, and he had yet to look directly at her.

"Thank God they're gone," Sheila said, stretching out her long legs. "Now we can relax. White folks"—she grimaced

—"will they never change? Can you imagine Hester telling me that I look just like Diahann Carroll?"

"We all look alike, don't you know?" Betty laughed. "Colored folks just looks like colored folks. Bet she thinks she paid you the supreme compliment."

Sarah suppressed a sigh of boredom. To her, Cathy's friends were all phonies. To hear them, whites were the dullest, most prejudiced lot ever. Yet for their affairs to be considered a success, whites had to be represented.

They, the Banning school's colored élite, had banded together with nothing in common except that they were middle class and light skinned—an answer to Banning's white students who kept them out of their inner circles. In turn they kept their darker-skinned sisters on the outside looking in.

Seeing Sarah in the doorway, Sheila raised her eyebrows. "Sarah, you here?" Then she turned her head, not expecting an answer. Sarah stared, resenting her. Sheila had nothing against her, she just didn't want her around.

"Haven't you had enough of us lamebrains?" Betty asked. "School's out. Be happy for your liberation."

Sarah flinched. The word *us* so clearly left her outside their circle—the circle that Lottie called "high-yeller pieces of turd."

"Wasn't that a grand affair." Cathy came to stand beside Sarah in the doorway. "We must have an encore."

"That will have to wait until we get back," Sheila said. "All we have time for now is to get ready and to get away."

"We have time." Cathy shook her hair back from her face. "What say, Milt—encore?"

"I'm with you, Cathy." Milt lay back on the couch, stretching his long skinny legs so that they almost reached the room's center. His watery eyes slid around Sarah to settle on Cathy. "Make me your stepping-stone," he said. "If you want encores every day until we leave—you got it."

"Heaven preserve us," Sheila sneered, her dislike for Milt obvious. But Cathy laughed. Milt's obsequious manner pleased her. It stamped him as her property. Cathy delighted in collecting friends—girls and boys—and making them her property. Sarah wondered how far along she had come with Fred. Had he, too, become one of Cathy's zombies?

"When we get back from our vacation, we'll be too tired," Cathy said. "So we should have another before we go."

Sarah walked over to the window and stood looking out. She hated Cathy's games. That's what she was playing when she spoke of teas and vacations in the Cape without inviting her. But then, Cathy had always been good at playing games.

Sarah gazed at a tanker sailing upriver, on whose deck tiny men scurried, securing ropes. Ropes as strong as the ties that bound her to Cathy, and which Cathy seemed so determined to break. Still, being overlooked for tea didn't constitute a break in lifelong friendship.

The tanker disappeared behind a clump of trees. The water in its wake spread, spread. Sarah kept staring down into the wake, imagining herself being lifted and, in slow motion, drifting down, down into its wake. She called out to the men. But they were busy with their tasks and didn't hear her. She called out again, louder, wanting them to turn and see her, to save her, pull her to them and tie her with the ropes—those strong ropes that held them together.

"Guess I'll be on my way," Sheila said, and a general confusion behind alerted her that Cathy's guests were leaving. "Yes, with all we have to do between now and then . . ."

Had they decided on another tea before? Did it matter? Sarah stared out of the window, listening to them whisper, laugh, and squeal in childish play as they went to the door. In her mind she saw them, their heads touching—fair, pretty Banning graduates—the smart set.

They had never become her friends, even though they had often come to the house to wait for Cathy. Now a sudden jealousy, a pain, pierced through Sarah, causing her to frown. Never had she felt so young, so inadequate. They were all her age—seventeen, eighteen—yet they were ladies while she had remained a child.

Sarah walked around the high-ceilinged room. She liked the way it was decorated—soft leather couch and chairs, porcelain lamps, and paintings by modern black artists on the walls. Mrs. Johnson called them the artists of the future.

Sarah's mother never hung paintings or pictures, preferring the stark cleanliness of white paint. Sarah wondered, if Lottie had been able to rent the apartment above this one when she had tried, where would she have placed the baby grand piano that Uncle Sam had given to Sarah?

Not in front of the window, where passing ships might distract Sarah. No, Lottie would have cleared space for Sarah's back to face the water—as her back faced the park in their apartment. Oh, the battles fought between Lottie and Uncle Sam over the placing of that piano. Uncle Sam had lost.

Sarah smiled thinking of her uncle, his big, broad black face, its tender eyes. How terrible never to have lived near a park, or water. How devastating to have lived all one's life locked into the innermost part of the inner city. Thinking of him sent her out into the hall, ready to leave.

Cathy came down the hall and stood facing her. "Sarah, really. Why didn't you call instead of just dropping in?"

"Since when have we had to call one another to say we're dropping in?" Sarah answered, staring back into the malicious blue eyes until they wavered.

"Sarah, I wanted to invite you to—this tea," Cathy said. "But I know how busy you always are. . . ."

"Yes," Sarah said. "I have been busy, with school, with practice—and helping my friend. But it's vacation time now, Cathy."

"Vacation time—well, what do you know. I guess you'll be practicing all summer, as usual." Cathy's tone needled Sarah, as it had been intended to do. But Sarah hadn't come to fight; she had come to salvage their friendship.

"My mother wants me to prepare myself this summer— I'm having some recitals this fall," Sarah said, then added, "But I—I'm tired, Cathy. I need a rest."

Sarah waited for Cathy's eyes to lighten with her usual exuberance, for her to say, "You've got to be tired. Why don't you ditch all that damn practicing and come on, let's go." Instead Cathy's eyes shifted, with a hint of hostility.

"Don't we all," she said. "I'm damn glad to be getting out of this town. Do you have any idea where you might go?"

Sarah hesitated. Cathy knew she had nowhere to go. But to suggest the Cape? To beg after she had already hinted? Sarah shook her head, shrugged her shoulders, and started up the hallway.

"Sarah? Honey, is that you?" Sarah turned to Mrs. Johnson, who had come into the hall. "I thought I recognized your voice. When did you get here?"

"Not long ago, Mrs. Johnson. And I'm just going."

"Without coming in to say hello?"

Mrs. Johnson and Cathy resembled each other strongly: Tall and thin, the same complexion, blond hair, and sooty blue eyes. The lines on Mrs. Johnson's face gave her a slightly haggard look, but her eyes were softer than her daughter's, gentler. Her appearance made the apartment suddenly become a friendlier place.

"I didn't know you were at home," Sarah answered.

"Yes, I'm here—locked up in my room."

"You were so quiet."

"It's the apartment, honey. Thank the Lord for big apartments. Imagine how crazy I'd be if I had to listen to Catherine's empty-headed friends chatter when I need to rest. How's Lottie?"

"Fine," Sarah answered, following her into the living room.

Sitting on a stuffed chair, Mrs. Johnson took a cigarette from the marble case on the table, lit it, inhaled deeply, then said, "You don't come around anymore. Why? I know school's out and you don't have to dash over here to save your friend from dropping out. But I'm still here."

Sarah squirmed at the implied criticism of Cathy. She deliberately changed the subject. "Aren't you working?" she asked.

"My first week of vacation," Mrs. Johnson said, taking off her slippers and wiggling her well-manicured toes. "What about Lottie? Is she taking time out this summer?"

"No, she's waiting for fall. I'm having recitals and she wants to be free to prepare for them."

Mrs. Johnson inhaled her cigarette. "She used to tell me about your recitals. Not anymore. Sarah, will you tell me what's wrong with that woman? She never comes by. Won't telephone. Refuses to speak to me when I call.

"Of course I don't get by to see her. I can't. As hard as I work I just don't have the energy to push through that gang that hangs around your stoop."

Honesty had always been Mrs. Johnson's strong point— even when the truth sounded ugly. And that truth did sound ugly—although Sarah had never accepted Lottie's unreasonable anger over it.

"Sarah," Mrs. Johnson said, "you know I tried to get Lottie an apartment in this house. So why's she mad at me? I didn't keep you all out. Sarah, there's lots of things I try to do for myself and don't succeed at.

"I didn't make this world. I came here and found it in this mess. When we were young, we—your mother and me —fought in movements to try to unscramble wrongs, to make things right—forever. But it's the 'man' out there that controls the checks and balances."

Sarah kept her eyes on the carpet. What could she say? She had heard both sides of the argument—if indeed there were two sides. Both Mrs. Johnson and Lottie Richardson agreed that they had fought "the system." They also agreed that some fights you win, others you lose. Sarah didn't understand the deep anger in Lottie that had caused the final break. She wanted to know, yet she didn't. She liked Mrs. Johnson and loved her mother. She didn't want to have to take sides.

Mrs. Johnson didn't expect her to. She changed the subject. "So you helped pull your friend through this term too." She blew out a cloud of smoke. "I must say, Sarah Richardson, you are a good friend. You're the best thing that ever happened to Lottie—and to us. You have the patience of a fool. Even you have to see that Cathy's not serious. I keep spending my money, sending her to good schools, and she just refuses to learn."

Sarah kept looking down at the carpet. She could feel Cathy's resentment from where she stood in the doorway. Finally Cathy said, "Why do you worry, Mother? I'm not planning on going through college. I intend to get married to someone rich and set you free."

"God forbid. It's not that overgrown simple-assed Milton who you've got drooling over you? I might want to be free," she joked. "But not that free." Then she abruptly changed the subject.

"Sarah, how are you doing in Juilliard?"

"Fine, Mrs. Johnson, just fine. I have some great instructors. They all believe in hard work—like Lottie. I enjoy it."

"Go on with your smart self, girl. There's nothing better than enjoying what's good for you."

"Yes. But I do get tired," Sarah admitted. "I work so hard. . . ."

"Work is what we womenfolk do best, child. You're lucky that you're doing what you want and love, and getting a scholarship for doing it. And you can always rest. . . . I bet you can hardly wait to get up to the Cape with us for the summer."

The sudden silence lasted a minute, then Sarah ventured, "Are you inviting me to the Cape, Mrs. Johnson?"

"Didn't Catherine invite you? I told her to." Mrs. Johnson's eyebrows rose. "Oh, I guess Catherine must have forgotten. Anyway, I am inviting you. We'll be leaving next weekend, so you had better get popping. . . ."

Sarah refused to look at Cathy. But she felt the anger rising—

"Mother, how dare you," Cathy cried.

For a moment blue eyes locked. Then Mrs. Johnson said, "And never mind that simple mother of yours, Sarah. I'll take care of her. I got lots to get off my mind anyway, so you tell her I'll be calling this very night. Just you go on and get ready."

Three

 Sarah felt such a tangle of emotions. First there was guilt for having accepted Mrs. Johnson's invitation against Cathy's and Lottie's wishes. She had begged. All the way home the weight of her betrayal grew. But as she sat at the dinner table, waiting for the phone to ring, fear dwarfed all other feelings. What excuse did she have to give?

No, Ma. I didn't ask. Yes, I did say yes, Ma. No, I didn't refuse. I didn't want to, Ma. I wanted to go. I wanted to go so very much. Then the hard part: *Ma, I have the right to decide. I'm seventeen—and I'm tired.*

Still the telephone remained silent. Sarah sat straining to be the first to hear the ring, and to tell Mrs. Johnson she had changed her mind after all. Why go through such agony just for a few weeks at Cape Cod?

Sarah kept her eyes fixed on her empty plate, away from her mother's I-want-to-know-what-you-know eyes.

"What's the matter, Puddin'?" Uncle Sam reached over the table to brush the back of his hand affectionately across her cheek.

"She's been that way since she came back from the Johnsons." Lottie's tone was one of exasperation. She prided herself on being able to see through her daughter's eyes into her brains, a feat that Sarah's looking at her plate prevented. "She's stuck so deep inside herself, you'll need pliers to pull her out."

"I told her not to go," Lottie said in her I-told-you-so tone. "Do you know, Sam? As much as Sarah's always helped that Cathy Johnson out, since school closed she ain't shown her butt around here. I know what's happening. But Sarah can't see for looking. That bunch that Cathy hangs with—I can't stand for them to come around. They got to be the most impolite young folks I ever did meet in my life. The girls don't do nothing but talk about boys and clothes, giggle, and act the fool. I bet they even smoke pot and drink."

"Come off it, Lottie," Uncle Sam chided her. "Kids nowadays and kids in your day's one and the same. Girls' titties get to sticking up on their chests and boys gets to scratching their groins and they get restless, ready to spread out. How old's Cathy? Seventeen? When you was that age you was about the same thing. What's more, Sarah here had been born."

"That was because I didn't have no sense and didn't have a mother to guide me," Lottie said.

"Lucky thing too," Sam kept on. "If Lottie hadn't gone out to get herself a li'l piece, what was we gonna do, Gladys? All these years, you and me—dried up and fruitless like we both done been spayed.

"Just look at our pretty Sarah—the sweetest and the brightest. You gonna make us famous—ain't you, Puddin'? Gladys, can't you see Sarah on stage, just a-bowing and smiling—looking out into the audience at us two old folks —with nothing holding us up 'cept some pride. . . ."

"Don't you be upholding that gal in such outrageous thought, Sam Gibbs." Aunt Gladys spoke more for insurance than from any real disagreement. "What if Sarah don't make it to be rich and famous? What if she settles for— other things?"

"Other things? Like what?" Uncle Sam's questions came like a warning growl deep in his throat.

"Like fallin' in love and makin' babies."

"Our Puddin's gonna be a star," Uncle Sam said, correcting her. "We ain't made sure she come this far—into Juilliard and all—to have her go making no babies—no, suh." He sopped up the last of his gravy with bread, his big, broad black face shining from earnestness. Then he had another thought. "Anyway, if she did, one of them babies'll be a star. I ain't about to leave this world until I see one of my kin light it up—no, suh. . . ."

"Oh, Sarah's gonna be famous," Lottie promised. "She mightn't be all that rich, but she'll sure be famous. I been a swimmer in this life—a strong swimmer. I gone against every tide and many a rough sea. If I didn't give her nothing else, I gave her that. No, she ain't about to end up with a bunch of babies—no way."

Sarah suppressed a sigh. She knew that their dreams were grounded in their shared experience: poverty. The poverty from which they had shielded her with every conscious effort. Poverty, the tightrope of their existence. One slip and down. Their every word, whether spoken in jest or seriousness, reflected this fear.

Gladys and Lottie Richardson had been abandoned as children. Gladys, the oldest, had a vague recollection of her mother. Lottie didn't. "Lord alone knows," Aunt Gladys often said when talking of her mother, "she might have gone out and got hit by a car. That's why she never got back." It was an idea Lottie took pleasure demolishing. "Both of them went out and got hit by the same car?"

The sisters were raised in foster homes until, at seventeen, Gladys had gone out into the world to find work, with a doctor and his wife, the job she still held. She had rented a room uptown in the building where Uncle Sam was the superintendent, a situation which he, too, still held.

Uncle Sam and Aunt Gladys had fallen in love and gotten married, and Aunt Gladys had moved into Uncle Sam's basement apartment. She had made it into a wonderful home, to which she had brought Lottie.

The building had been a grand old building then and remained decent even in a neighborhood where most others had become havens for addicts, or had fallen in on themselves from vandalism.

Bright Lottie, frisky Lottie, was starved for affection. She had fallen for the first boy she met. Both were sixteen. From their union Sarah had been born. Lottie had never told the boy's name. Maybe she didn't even remember it. Her operational words were "Never look back." In time those words were replaced by "get ahead." By then Lottie had fallen in love with work.

Aunt Gladys had sent her sister through junior high, then high school, and cared for her even up to her first civil service job as a clerk. Getting ahead for Lottie meant studying and going to night school, taking special courses that kept her away from home. That hadn't mattered to Uncle Sam and Aunt Gladys—they loved their "Puddin'." When Lottie had taken Sarah out of the basement apartment to Parkview, they grieved.

"Now, that Cathy." Lottie wiped her mouth with her napkin. "I sure hope she loves babies. Because she's gonna end up with a mess of them."

Uncle Sam scowled. "How you sound, Lottie! Children is children. They goes their way doing what they got to do."

"Sam, you ever take a good look at Cathy? That girl's a witch. Not that she can help it, given the mother she's got. But I sure am glad she don't come around like she used to. I didn't want my child end up getting hurt."

"That ain't something you can stop," Uncle Sam said. "That's what friends are for. To learn love and pain from one another. Just on account of you mad at Clarice, don't take it out on her kid. I ain't taking sides with you against Clarice. What right you got to faulting her on account she decided to move—and did?"

" 'Cause Lottie couldn't," Aunt Gladys said, with a note of smug satisfaction. "But then a friend, a good friend, won't never move into a place where her best friend's likely to be kept out of."

"Gladys, didn't Lottie move out of our house the first chance she got?" Sam pointed out.

"Sure did," Aunt Gladys nodded.

"Seems to me," Uncle Sam went on, "we black folks just keeps a-moving away from one another. Don't it seem that way to you?"

"Sure do." Aunt Gladys nodded again.

Lottie refused to hear again those arguments about her having taken Sarah from their home. She closed her face, rose from the table, and marched into the living room. The rest followed.

Sitting stiff-backed at the piano, Sarah started off with her uncle's favorite, Rachmaninoff's piano concerto. Pride radiated from them. Uncle Sam adjusted his three hundred pounds on her mother's fragile antique chair. The chair creaked and Lottie's mouth winced. Aunt Gladys sat upright and proper with a placid smile softening her plain black face. Sarah, facing the wall, saw them all, played to them all, while she sat, her back held taut, waiting for the telephone to ring.

"Just listen to my gal," Uncle Sam said, sighing when she had ended. Sarah immediately went into her Aunt Gladys's favorite, Minuet in G by Paderewski. That had been her first piece, learned while she was still living with her aunt and uncle. It brought Aunt Gladys memories she loved.

Beethoven's Fifth, Sarah played for Lottie. Lottie took a strange pride in that accomplishment. Whenever she met a parent at school, or at a concert hall, she prefaced her remarks with: "Yes—my daughter plays Beethoven's Fifth. . . ."

Sarah played with more gusto than usual, hitting the stronger notes, pressing down on the bass, letting her hands fly relentlessly over the keyboard, then coming to a crashing crescendo. Still she heard the telephone ring and jumped to her feet.

"No, no, Puddin'," her uncle said. "Let Lottie answer. Come on, now, let's do our number."

Dutifully Sarah sat, watching her mother leaving the room. She played Duke Ellington's "Sophisticated Lady," then "Take the 'A' Train." And while her Uncle Sam and Aunt Gladys hummed along, snapping their fingers in time, Sarah strained to hear her mother in the foyer, talking, talking, rage in her voice.

When Lottie walked back into the room, Sarah's hands froze. Her uncle kept on singing and humming, just snapping his fingers, expecting Sarah to go on. Sarah sat, her head bowed, waiting for her mother to speak. And Lottie let her wait.

Finally Sarah heard her name. It sounded like the snap of a whip.

"Sarah! That call came from Clarice Johnson." She stood waiting. Sarah bowed her head. "She told me that she asked you to go with her to Cape Cod next weekend. She said you said yes."

Even the air stopped circulating in the silent room. Sarah tried to regulate her breathing. Sarah had been invited to the Cape. She wanted to go. Furthermore, she intended to go. The firmness of her decision surprised Sarah. Never before had she gone against Lottie's authority. Yet in one day she had done so, twice.

Now, however, Sarah's heart hammered and her face quivered. She knew she had to take a stand.

"You didn't ask me if it was all right, Sarah? You didn't try to find out if I had other plans?"

"What other plans, Mother?" She looked up, into her mother's eyes. For seconds they stared, unblinking, at each other. "I know you want me to stay here in the city and practice. But I'm tired, Mother. I need a rest. Do you understand that?"

"Aren't we all tired?" her mother answered.

"I have never been anywhere in my life, Mother. All I ever do is study and practice, and practice and study. . . ."

"The rest of us work all the time, too, Sarah—hard. We never complain, because in this life, rest isn't what's important, Sarah. It's getting ahead."

When Lottie spoke those words no one went against her. She had a hundred arguments with which to support them. Hearing them this time, Sarah stood tall, squaring her shoulders. She was taller than her mother, her face more serious. She drew the seriousness into her eyes and directed it at Lottie. "Ma, when I left here this afternoon, I had no intention of going against your wishes. The invitation came unexpectedly. I didn't have time to think. I said yes, because I want to go, Ma. I don't want to go against your wish— ever. So don't try to prevent me."

Lottie returned the unblinking stare, but only for a few seconds. Then she closed her face. Uncle Sam, seeing the closed face and sensing her anguish, said, "Where you say you was going, Sarah? The Cape? Cape Cod? Sounds purty. Wasn't you there once, Lottie? That time when Clarice's husband up and died so sudden and all? When you come back from the funeral, I recall you saying it was a real nice place. Never can tell, Puddin' might have a real good—"

"Sam Gibbs, I'll not have you interfering in my life." Lottie spun around venting her anger on him. "It's hard enough raising a fatherless child. I've done everything I know how . . ."

"We all done what we know how," Uncle Sam corrected his sister-in-law gently. He knew her well, knew how hard it was for her to accept a challenge to her authority.

But Aunt Gladys had heard nothing except her sister's attack on her husband. "We sure have," she said, coming to his support. "Best proof, we living in that same basement apartment since Puddin' was born. And I'm workin' hard same's I did when I brought your butt in that same apartment. We had a chance to buy us a pretty old house—out on the island. But, no"—now she turned her resentment against her husband—"Sam wasn't going nowhere. Had to stay in that old dump, jawboning with his bummy friends."

"Now, Gladys." Uncle Sam shifted painfully on the squeaking chair. "You know that we—you and me—done decided that that li'l bit of money we'd done saved up made more sense tending to Puddin's education. Now, I don't want to hear a lot of bellyaching on account we settled on looking out for Puddin'. Makes no more sense than that simple sister of yours trying to make our girl feel bad on account of Clarice moving."

"Don't you be putting my sister down." Aunt Gladys

stood up and pushed her face down to his. "Just look at us now, Sam Gibbs. That ole gang of yours all dead—every last one of 'em."

"Stop it, stop it," Lottie cried. "You got it wrong, Sam. My grievance with my daughter don't have a damn thing to do with Clarice moving from here. What I care if she got a place on the river? What gets me is she thinks she's too damn good to come around this building where she used to live."

"Lottie," Uncle Sam liked to have a place for everything and liked to see everything in its place. "Every Thursday, right as rain, we—Gladys and me—makes our way down-town to see you and Puddin'. When's the last time we seen either one a you come uptown to see about us?"

"Sam, you got to be kidding," Lottie protested. "Do you really expect us—expect me to send my child uptown to see you in that broken-down dangerous old neighborhood?"

Uncle Sam chuckled. He spread his arms wide, catching her eyes. "Aha—see that?"

Lottie sputtered. She hated being caught wrong. She looked around, stared into each face, then stalked out of the room.

Lottie's face remained closed. Mother and daughter barely spoke up to the day Sarah left. Then Sarah found that she had escaped the animosity of their apartment only to be trapped in the snake-pit atmosphere of the city-to-Cape drive remarkable for its silence: Cathy and her mother had quarreled too, and Sarah knew it had to do with her.

So she added to the silence by staring out of the window

in the backseat of the car, at the countryside—the stretches of woods, the storybook barns where cows stood in barn-yards, as motionless as though in paintings. Sarah longed to take flight in one of her fantasies. She wanted to escape the turbulence raging in the car through the lightness of spirit which her fantasies allowed her. But the grim silence had deeper roots than the petty anger between Sarah and her mother.

Lottie and Sarah had always wanted the same things for Sarah. Mrs. Johnson's relationship with Cathy, the rebel with or without a cause, had never been easy. Mrs. Johnson had spent Cathy's lifetime trying to mold dreams that Cathy rejected. She had tried to force Cathy to take piano lessons. When Cathy refused to practice, she had substituted the violin, which Cathy had promptly sold. For a long time she had tried to induce Cathy to take ballet. But Cathy saw all of Mrs. Johnson's efforts as a means to make her measure up to Sarah—and that Cathy refused to tolerate.

Cathy had always been a free spirit—a law unto herself. Neither Mrs. Johnson's love, nor her anger, nor her remark-able wit had been strong enough to force Cathy to conform.

Why had she come, when she knew Cathy didn't want her, Sarah asked herself. Because of Fred? Yes, she wanted to be near him. But was it worth the anger, the hostility, which—on the seemingly endless drive—had taken on a life of its own?

Cathy sat in smug satisfaction, pleased with the discomfort she had caused. Mrs. Johnson drove in stiff-backed determination. Sarah kept gazing out at the scenery. They ate in fast-food restaurants, silently, and drove on in silence.

From time to time Sarah dozed, then awoke to gaze out at the sameness of the landscape.

In the early evening they crossed from the mainland into Cape Cod, to find themselves wedged in bumper-to-bumper traffic. Finally Mrs. Johnson turned off into a narrow, tree-lined road. Immediately the quality of silence changed.

The air became softer, sweet with the smell of the sea. Fog smothered the rays of the soon-to-be-setting sun with the wispiness of multicolored chiffon that made the air hazy. At one instant, fog moved toward them, threatening to surround them, then seeped into the bordering woods to settle as shadow. The road curved around into a lane bordered with petunias, behind which a field of tea roses hugged the ground, yellow buds spreading out for miles.

They pulled up before an old Cape Cod saltshaker type house of white cedar-block shingles. On its steep roof a chimney protruded. Rambling roses, ivy, and other colorful vine flowers covered the front porch and climbed up to the second floor, giving to it the look of a patchwork quilt.

Drained from the long, emotional drive, Mrs. Johnson slumped over the wheel. Cathy jumped out and bounded up the steps of the porch, where an old woman sat in a rocking chair. "Grandma, Grandma," she shouted with the return of her charm. The old woman's face lit up with pleasure.

"Lordy." The woman stood up from the old rocker. "I thought that this day would never get here." She was frail, black, and dressed in an old-fashioned long dress, which made her appear to have stepped out of another time. "Seems to me like some one of you ought to have known how lonesome an old lady can get in a big house all by herself and hurry the time getting here."

"Did the best I could," Mrs. Johnson said as she got out of the car. "Mother, I declare," she said as she walked stiff and aching up the steps. "Thinking of you and missing you takes up most of my waking moments. I miss this house— the peace. . . . Nobody ever told me that working so hard and getting this tired was in my cards."

"Clarice, you the one holding the cards." The woman grinned, baring teeth brown with age. "It's up to you the way you wants to play 'em. The house been here. I'm here. Don't make no sense my little family living in that far-off, fast-moving city, when they can settle here."

"What about work, lady?" Mrs. Johnson pushed back the white soft hair and kissed the lined black forehead. "Mother, I love you, love you, love you. But leave New York! My work! Never."

The old woman shrugged. "Guess it's best having you a li'l time than not at all." She stretched out her hand to take Sarah's and pull her up the steps to the porch. "Who's this pretty li'l lady we got here with us?"

"Sarah? Pretty?" Cathy arched her eyes in disbelief.

"Sure is. Sarah? Pretty name too."

"Mother invited her," Cathy said.

"I reckoned somebody did. Serious, she seems to me. Not like the others you brings here."

"Don't count your blessings yet, Mother." Mrs. Johnson laughed. "The gang's on the way."

"Oh, my dear . . ." Old hands fluttered over the ruffles at her neck. "Anyhow, Sarah, glad you're here. Whosoever is on the way, you'll be a welcome addition. Never can tell, you and Catherine might get to be friends."

"But they are friends," Mrs. Johnson said. "Have been for years."

"From the way Cathy said that you—"

"Sarah's Lottie's daughter," Mrs. Johnson said. "You do remember my friend Lottie?"

"Lottie . . . Lottie." The woman looked Sarah over. "How do one ever forget Lottie—that wonderful friend on whose shoulders we all cried when Li'l Jason passed. I'll never forget her. Still, by the time Big Jason went, she wasn't up here, was she? I remember looking for her. How is she?"

"Fine as ever." Mrs. Johnson looked away from Sarah. "Active as ever. You know she's a big-time supervisor— head of her department at the state unemployment bureau."

"Supervisor, huh? I'm sure." The elder Mrs. Johnson nodded her head, kept nodding her head. "A strong, deserving woman—an understanding woman."

"Sarah's quite a kid too." Mrs. Johnson looked back at Sarah. "I don't know what we'd have done without her helping your granddaughter pass through school. She's Cathy's best friend—the best friend Cathy'll ever have."

"Then you gotta have a mess of patience." The grandmother laughed, grabbing hold of Cathy's hand. "Never you mind, my wild one. I still loves you—you just like your granddaddy. . . . Now, how many did you say you was bringing up here this time?"

"Five."

"That many?"

"Yes, Grandma. I have two boyfriends now," Cathy bragged, hoping to shock her grandmother.

"I hope they both gentle folks."

"I hope she knows what she's doing," Mrs. Johnson remarked, sarcasm clearly underlining her displeasure. "One is that Milton James. She brought him last year."

"Milton James? Can't recall . . ."

"Betty and Sheila are coming," Cathy said.

"Seems I remember them."

"And Betty's bringing her boyfriend—Jody McCoy."

"My dear. A crowd. They're gonna have to double up. I'm expecting folks too. But Sarah here, she can have the brown-and-tan room and—"

"Sarah!" Cathy's voice rose. "Grandma, that's Sheila's room."

Her grandmother wrinkled her brows playfully, but determination flashed through faded brown eyes. "Correction, miss, Sheila owns no space in this house. I allowed her to stay in that room the last time. We had enough space. Like I said, this year I'm having other folks."

She stood tall, that tiny, frail lady. She was the smallest of any of them but she stood straighter. "You remember the Armands, don't you? Madame Armand and her son—good friends to the Dixons. They're passing through. Son's got business here in the States. She's along to keep him company. I was hoping you'd get here at the same time. But seems he got held up in Washington, don't you know."

"You can't do this, Grandmother," Cathy cried, her face flushed with anger. "I won't let you."

Sarah looked away from them. She gazed down the

length of the porch to the door at the other end. She looked over the porch to the garden of long-stemmed American Beauty roses, growing tall, along the path of the house, then gazed in wonder at the woods, which towered like a great wall alongside the path.

"Cathy." The old woman's calm voice caught her attention and Sarah looked to see her holding on to Cathy's chin, refusing her permission to turn away. "Now, if you wants to give up your room to whatever friend, then go on ahead. You got my permission. The boys, they can set up in the downstairs playroom. I've got enough cots. And if the girls don't like the idea of sharing with you, then they got the blue room."

"I promised Milton his private room," Cathy wailed. "Mother, how can a boy like Milt sleep on a cot?"

"Easy," Mrs. Johnson quipped. "Just make sure he opens it." For a moment mother and daughter exchanged hard glances.

The old woman ruffled Cathy's hair. "They'll manage, honey. Boys can surprise you with they know-how." Taking Sarah's hand, she pulled her. "Come, let me show you to your room."

"I have to get my bags," Sarah protested.

"Alicia and Cathy can bring them." A wicked gleam shone in the old woman's eyes as she pulled Sarah into the house with surprisingly strong hands.

The inside of the house surprised Sarah. It seemed so spacious, considering the modest exterior. They entered a high-ceilinged foyer that ended with the stairs. Behind the stairs an open door revealed a complex of rooms that carried the eyes back into seemingly endless space. "That's the first addition to this house. Big Jason built that." She chuckled. "That's why we calls this a rambling house, don't you know. But come."

Sarah stepped into the first room opening from the foyer, a vast dining room with a long table that could seat thirty, yet took only a little of the room's space. The table had been partially set. Gleaming silverware and shining glasses stood out against its dark brown mahogany. The sideboards, too, were of the same dark wood, their glass-topped doors exposing generations of china and glasses. Around the room large tables bearing gigantic vases of long-stemmed flowers —American Beauty roses, gladiolas of different hues of lavender. Care was evident in everything—even to the hardwood floors, polished then waxed, shining beneath scatter rugs.

"Someone's always adding wings to this old house," the woman said. Her eyes kept searching Sarah's face, appreciating her admiration.

While speaking she had pulled Sarah from the dining room through an old-fashioned butler's pantry and into an immense kitchen, where an old-fashioned gas stove and oven shared the wall with a wood-burning iron stove. Above the stove, from a ceiling rack, dozens and dozens of iron and aluminum pots hung. A round butcher-block table with matching chairs made a coffee nook. Then Sarah was being pulled again, outside to a wraparound porch, then back into a large apartment made up of two bedrooms with a luxury bath.

"This wing my daughter-in-law had built when she got

herself her decorator's job. She spends much of her time here when she comes, but I have to ask her to give it up for my out-of-town guests, don't you know." One wall of the apartment looked out over the side path and the woods. In the darkening day the woods looked brooding, mysterious. "This is the last addition of this old house," the woman said. "There'll be no more."

Back in the dining room Sarah wandered into the adjacent room, a parlor, the smallest room she had seen. It had been cut away to make room for the wing. Yet it retained a coziness, nestling next to the dining room. Two velvet sofas faced each other in front of a big fireplace. Chairs of less significance were scattered around. But Sarah, seeing the baby grand piano standing near the door leading out to the foyer, lost interest in all else.

She had a friend. A dear, dear friend whatever happened. No, she didn't intend to play and bring Cathy's hostility out to clog up the atmosphere. But how good to know that it was here. How very good.

"Downstairs is the playroom where the boys will be," the woman said, leading Sarah up the steps. "And we have an attic too. We store things up there that we have no use for but we love too much to throw out. On this floor"—they had come to the landing—"we live."

She opened the door to a room. "This here is my room," she said. A smell of old perfume and pine blew into their faces. It was a large room with furniture of light-colored pine, highly waxed. They looked around, then once again she pulled Sarah, this time to the opposite end of the floor.

"And this"—she was showing her flare for drama as she pushed open the door—"is the brown-and-tan room."

"Ooooooh." Sarah stepped into the largest room of the house and the most magnificent she had ever seen. It appeared to be a combination library, study, and bedroom. It also had a bathroom of its own. The furniture was massive —the huge desk, with leather seated chair, bookcases, chests, framed photographs and paintings, were all of dark wood. It had been a man's room, without doubt. And despite the fact that there were no men in the house, it was polished with the same, if not greater, conscientiousness as the furniture in the other parts of the house. Breathtaking. The glowing room caught and reflected the fading glow of sunlight that came through the floor-to-ceiling French doors, which opened onto a terrace. "Mrs. Johnson, you shouldn't have. . . ."

"Mama Dear," the sweet-faced woman said. "Call me Mama Dear. It is a dream room," she said, smiling at the amazement in Sarah's face. "I knew you'd appreciate this room the second I set eyes on you. It's a serious room. . . .

"That Sheila? She's okay. But she don't have poetry in her face, don't you know. I don't reckon she stayed in here long enough last year to see it. She'd get up mornings, off she'd go. Couldn't break away from the rest of them long enough to stay and give it a good look."

Sarah kept looking around, knowing why Cathy wanted it for the one she considered her "best friend" now. Stepping into the room had been like stepping into another time: paintings and photographs, the brass reading lamps, the wide bed with its copper posts. History looked down at her through the eyes of the paintings and photographs. She stared back. Did she really want to be in this room? Had she come this far from Lottie's rigid rules to spend days, nights, under such scrutiny?

". . . calling herself having a good time." Mama Dear shook her head. "That's Cathy and her bunch. Air. Some folks bring only air to a place. They come, they go, like a draft. Then some folks leaves a bit of themselves—their spirit, don't you know. A bit of the soul. . . ." She smiled up at the portraits, the photographs. Her body heaved. She looked at Sarah.

"Cathy's friends, now, they follow Cathy. They don't know that Cathy ain't so free as she's wild—her grandpa's own child.

"Li'l Jason was always a good, mild-mannered child. The sweetest little boy. He was born right here—in this house, don't you know. Wildness skipped his generation, but it settled in on Cathy." She stared out into space a moment then. "I love Cathy. . . ."

Sarah walked over to the French doors, then stepped out on the terrace. She looked down at the wraparound porch, then over the path into the woods. Sarah had always thought that she alone understood Cathy. It startled her that Mama Dear understood her too—perhaps even more than she did.

A branch of a big tree at the edge of the woods stretched over the path to tap the corner of the terrace. It caught Sarah's attention. She looked from the branch to its trunk, trying to see beyond the trunk into the woods. Interlocked branches and the rapidly fading daylight prevented her.

"Those woods are fascinating," she said.

"You mean mysterious, don't you?" Mama Dear came to stand beside her on the terrace. "Walk into them and you're liable never to walk out—not the same, at any rate."

"Wonderful." Sarah laughed. Her eyes shone. She adored the little woman, the mischief that lit the old eyes. "I'll go in while I'm here. How many have you lost in there?"

"Fair to middling." The old woman grinned.

"How many have gotten lost and not come out at all?"

"Anyone who gets lost in there—gets lost," Mama Dear answered. Sarah laughed. Humor and mischief in older people was so refreshing. "Go on in. Explore. But never forget that I warned you. Now, when you get to that pond—"

"Oh, a pond? A large one?"

"Fair to middling, considering ponds around here," the old woman teased. "Throw a stone in it, make a wish—if it ripples, that wish will come true."

"Is that so?"

"Just as sure as you're standing there." Then, at the doubt on Sarah's face, she shrugged. "Anyway, we got to be wishing our wishes come true—or why wish at all?"

They laughed together. "Have those woods always been there?" Sarah asked.

"You mean did we plant them. Folks don't go around planting woods like that. They goes around cutting them down. Those been here since I came—and I been here for well over fifty years."

Cathy came into the room then. She had brought up one of Sarah's bags. The tall platinum blonde who came in with her brought the other. "Mother made me help Alicia bring your bags," Cathy said. "From the weight of them one would think you came to spend a year."

"Your grandmother's been telling me that she's been here over fifty years," Sarah said, determined to force Cathy to act pleasant.

"That's right," Mama Dear said. "I been knowing Alicia's folks that long. I known her great-grandfather. They was the first family to greet us—Jason and me—when Old Master Dixon brought us north. Alicia's great-grandfather and Master Dixon, they used to farm together—grew asparagus, before the sea trade took over on the Cape."

"Thank you for bringing my bag," Sarah said to the bronzed blond girl.

"Alicia's no end of help to me. My caretaker, ain't you, Alicia?"

"I work and get paid for working," Alicia said.

"Alicia," Mama Dear whispered. "I won't tell that I know Clarice hired you to keep me from falling and breaking my neck."

"That amounts to all I do," Alicia said to Sarah. "She exhausts me. I keep looking at her, waxing floors, polishing them, while I sit around reading or doing my homework."

"There's a good girl." Mama Dear whispered. "She don't like to help me out on account she don't want me to feel the helpless old lady."

"What's all the whispering about?" Mrs. Johnson said, coming into the room.

"Mama Dear was just telling me she's been here for fifty years. I thought Cathy's father's folks were all from Massachusetts," Sarah explained.

"No indeed." Mama Dear shook her head. "I'm from the Deep South—Mississippi . . . and I mean *from*—with no hankering to go back." She walked over to the big leather-seated chair at the desk.

"We—me and Big Jason, Big Red we called him—got chased out of Mississippi on account of he had done killed the sheriff." She sat down, looked around at them, and they dutifully walked to stand around her.

"Yes, he had to leave on account he killed a man. Me—I left because I loved that man!

"Big Red and Nathan, his brother, was some wild boys. They father being half white, they come by it natural. Evil. They grandfather was said to be the master of a plantation. He had killed blacks, strung them up on account he took on the role of God. Guess Nathan and Jason figured as grandsons of God, they had inherited that role by divine right. Yes'm. Being of white blood and ignorant in the South can make even the good Lord Jesus into a brute. Wild without being free—now, that's a terr'ble place to be.

"They was bad. Them boys robbed, talked back to white folks. See, we blacks in the South had to step out of the way of white folks on the road. But them brothers stood in white folks' way, stared them down, jawboned like they ain't had no sense, then spat after them when they passed on. Folks knew they had to die. That them 'crazy niggers' lived past their youth made them into mighty 'lucky niggers.'

"But them brothers loved black women. They loved their

black mama. They loved black girls coming up, and they loved black women when they got grown. So it had to be a lie when the sheriff come and took Nathan out of his house on account of, as he said, Nathan had touched a white woman.

"So happens Nathan had been home with the fever. His woman had stayed home that week just to look after him. She 'splained all that to the sheriff. Still they took Nathan, fevered like he was, and strung him up."

Cathy had gone to stand before a blown-up photograph of her grandfather. Mrs. Johnson sat at the edge of the bed. Alicia stood politely, her round blue eyes staring at Mama Dear. Obviously, they had all heard this tale before. But Sarah hadn't, and she asked in disbelief, "Lynching a man for no reason?"

"Shows you ain't up on your most recent history," the tiny woman scolded Sarah. "It ain't been that far back in time when them crackers lynched black folks like they thought that blacks might go out of season. The only reason they ain't is because we weren't all that easy to kill. Then those communists, you know, they started up such a stink, don't you know, about the Scottsboro Boys. Then next here comes Martin Luther King. That sort of got the government to set on their backs—for a spell. But ain't nothing to say they ain't gonna start trying again when they got the mind to.

"It's all about power, don't you see. Put power in the hands of small-minded folks and they do things that the good Lord ain't even thought up yet.

"Anyway, the sheriff killed Big Red's brother and Big Red killed hisself a sheriff. He had to get out of the South. And me—I had to get out too. Funny thing, don't you know, that Big Red laid a kiss on my brow when I was a li'l bit of a thing. From that day I walked in his footsteps. He had to go, so I had to go.

"Got me a job in St. Louis, scrubbing floors in a office building after it done close nights. And just to show that when the Lord limps up to His next move—ain't nobody His equal.

"So happen that the building I worked in's the same building Master Dixon had come to for his meeting in St. Louis. And it so happen that on that night of Master Dixon's meeting a robber decided to rob some poor soul. It so happens that on that night, too, Jason come to pick me, after I finished my chores.

"The robber chooses Master Dixon for his mark. My Jason stops the man and saves Master Dixon's life. And so—here we are. A humdinger. Jason ain't never cared about no white folks. He cared less if he seen them getting robbed, or killed. Yet this night he felt moved to stop that thief. He grabs the man, takes away his knife, turns him upside down, and shakes his money out of him. My Jason was a big man. That robber couldn't take off fast enough."

"Was the man black?" Sarah asked.

"No'm. Was a white man. Tell you, when the good Lord catch up, he gives an eye on detail. Jason might never have paid him no mind if he was black. . . . Anyway, Master Dixon looks up at Big Red and say, 'What the hell you doing hangin' round here?' Damn fool question. Big Red turns on him:

" 'I'm laying low on account of a lynching,' he says. 'My lynching. I killed me a cracker sheriff in Mississippi, and I ain't got nothing against killing me another cracker right here in St. Louis.'

"They stand toe to toe eyeing one another and just like that a brotherhood sprung up between them. 'You want work?' Master Dixon ask.

" 'That's like askin' if I wants to eat,' Big Jason answered.

" 'What can you do?'

" 'Anythin' and everythin' that any man can do—only better.'

"Right on the spot Master Dixon hires him. And brung him—us—north to this house.

"So you see, Sarah, this is a dream house—my dream house. Although I didn't know nothing about dreams like that until it happen to me.

"Jason and me, we married in this house. We made that happen. We thrown pebbles into the pond and wished it to happen. After all, we were getting on in age.

"And we wished for our boy too. Prudence and me had our boys right here in this house, only months apart. Li'l Jason and Alvin. We christened them right in that pond. . . ."

Cathy walked over to her grandmother as the story neared its end, and for the first time since leaving the city a pleasant expression eased her face. "Grandma, I want you to tell about the time—"

At that moment shrieks of laughter and the blowing of car horns came through the window. Cathy ran from the room and they heard her footsteps racing down the stairs. Her friends had arrived.

Four

 Not wanting to break the spell woven by the tales of the impish old woman, Sarah decided to unpack before going down to greet the others. And when she did, she walked into the sound of Betty's irritating babyish voice: "Grandmother, I missed you. Whatever would I do if I didn't have you to come to on the first week of July?"

And Cathy: "Grandma, meet Fred—Fred Hamilton. You've heard about the big-time college basketball star? This is Fred."

Fred: "Hello, Mrs. Johnson. Nobody ever told me how young and beautiful you really are."

Mama Dear: "Go on with you. Where did Cathy find herself such a boy? Studying good manners, and good looking too."

Cathy: "You remember Milt from last year, don't you,

Grandma? And this is Jody—Betty's friend. I told you that Betty was bringing her new friend."

Their voices, their excitement, touched Sarah. Suddenly she was glad they were there. So what if they didn't like her? Some of the fault might be with her. If so, she intended to change—to charm them. She had studied the art from Cathy. She had come for a vacation. She intended to have one.

She stepped into the dining room with a smile on her face, and stood looking at them swirling around Mama Dear. They had filled her arms with presents, delighting her. It was the first time Sarah had even seen Betty's boyfriend, Jody, a stocky, short-limbed youth with the kindly face of an English bull. Fred, tall, broad, handsome, in his white cotton knit pullover and black slacks. Milt James wore tight jeans with a turtleneck cotton knit, which made his long, too-lean frame too long and too lean.

Sheila had come too. Sarah hadn't heard her voice from the stairs and had hoped that she might have fallen, broken a leg—something. Sarah hated Sheila, perhaps because she appeared to have replaced her as Cathy's best friend. But more because of Sheila's disdain of her, the tilt of her aristocratic head, the condescending sneer she passed off as a smile—the smile that she now turned on when she saw Sarah coming into the room.

"Cathy, you didn't tell me you had invited Sarah."

"I didn't," Cathy retorted. "Mother did. What's more"—Cathy's tight smile, her tone, telegraphed her malicious intent—"Grandma gave her the brown-and-tan room."

"Oh . . . ?" Sheila responded, receiving the message.

They all had heard the message. The atmosphere in the room tightened even before Sheila's gaze slipped over Sarah.

Mrs. Johnson, too, had heard the message and, knowing her daughter so well, tried to lighten the moment. "Cathy, why don't you show your friends their rooms—now!" She smiled. "I know you can hardly wait for what Mother has fixed for dinner."

All eyes were averted as they filed past Sarah in the doorway, even Fred's. But he did attempt to joke. "Lead the way, Cathy," he cried. "I yam a very tired man. What's more, I yam a very hungry one." Nobody laughed. Cathy had already set the tone.

They scattered through the house. Mama Dear stood beside the table. "Don't you pay them no mind, honey." She took Sarah's hand and massaged it. "Whatever they say, they ain't nothing but bits of fluff."

Mama Dear kept looking over her presents heaped on the dining-room table, trying to still the pleasure that had taken over her face. Finally she gave in to it. "What's an old lady to do?" She spread her arms out in a helpless gesture. "I can't lie. I enjoy this."

Sarah's face burned. Embarrassed. She hadn't brought a present. She hadn't known to bring one. She, too, looked over the presents while hearing the laughter of the others, their joking, their ability to enjoy being together and being here. She sighed. An unfinished feeling filled her. Up to that moment she had always enjoyed being called serious minded.

Alicia helped Mama Dear serve dinner course by course. "Don't know what I'd do without that girl." Mama Dear looked at the blond girl fondly.

"Alicia's grandpa and Big Jason got along well. When Big Red started giving his speeches and preaching the ills in this country, Master Dixon, he had him talking from one end of the East Coast to another. And her grandpa got all tied up with the boats and the fish."

"I always wait until my second day before Mother will let me help out," Mrs. Johnson explained when Alicia and Mama Dear were in the kitchen. "My mother-in-law can be a very stubborn lady. I wanted to hire a full-time cook and housekeeper. But Mother insists that she's the best cook on this side of the Atlantic. I agree. She also believes she's stronger today than when she was sixteen. What can I do? I had to force her to take on Alicia. I convinced her that she had a duty to help out a young student. Thank God. Now I have a friend to look out for the old girl and report to me once a week."

The dinner started with clam chowder—the best Sarah had ever tasted. Mama Dear refused to sit with them. She insisted, "Time to eat food's when it's hot, so don't wait for me." She and Alicia kept bringing food: a mixed seafood grill amazed Sarah. Never before had she tasted the difference between fresh fish from the sea and fresh fish from fish markets. Next they had pasta. Only when the dessert had finished baking, and Mama Dear had set hot peach cobbler on the table, did she sit down.

The meal had taken hours to prepare and almost the same time to consume. They all ate seconds and might have asked for thirds if Milt James hadn't pushed away from the table. "Whoa. We can't be too greedy. We got a big night ahead."

"Not so fast." Mrs. Johnson restrained them as they made a dash from their seats. "We have to help Alicia clear the table."

"What for?" Milt asked. "The girl gets paid, doesn't she?"

Mama Dear squinted down the table at him. "Young man, do I know you?"

"Sure you do, Mrs. Johnson. I came up last year. You got to remember."

"Perhaps last year you didn't act so crude," Mama Dear snapped. Milt's face reddened. He looked toward Sarah and for the first time their eyes met. She fought to hold back the satisfaction she felt at the rebuke. Couldn't. His watery blue eyes hardened with such hatred, it made Sarah's heart leap, then flutter against the wall of her chest.

They all moved to clear the table and they did it briskly. Then left. Sarah stayed in the kitchen to help Alicia wipe and put away the dishes. The others went to dress. When Sarah came back into the dining room, they were ready to leave.

"Sarah, aren't you going with them?" Mrs. Johnson asked. Cathy spun around to confront her mother. For seconds mother and daughter glared at each other, then Mrs. Johnson asked Sarah, "Do you want to go with them?" Sarah shook her head no.

"I—I'm tired. I'll rest up tonight." They walked out of the house and went to their cars. Sarah heard their motors start up as she walked up the stairs and into her room. But once inside the brown-and-tan room, she moved about agitatedly. She had come uninvited by Cathy, so she ought to have expected this. But knowing didn't relieve the pain. Standing at the oversized desk she fought back tears. Wiped those that came, with the back of her hand, and focused at the large painting hanging over the desk.

Master Dixon, proud, haughty, with heavy jowls. A thick mustache hung over his lips, giving an aspect of sternness. Beside it the portrait of Prudence Dixon—another generation's ideal of gentility: fragile, blond, wearing a chiffon dress, a wide-brimmed horsehair hat flopping over her face; a nearby basket of roses highlighted the rosiness of her cheeks.

Yet in the photographs, brown and faded from age, Mr. Dixon appeared to be a gentle man, humble and loving. Prudence, a buxom woman with mischievous laughter that lit up her face, had a strong peasantlike neck and a massive head of hair. On all the pictures they had taken together, they gave off the feel of two people in love—with each other, with life, and with their work.

Portraits and photographs—the history of lives already lived. One was a blown-up photograph of Big Red, the picture Cathy had been admiring earlier. He had indeed been a big man, broad of face, freckled. He stared out of that picture, his eyes living still, in their anger. On one panel were photographs of two boys: one white, platinum, the other brown, with tightly curled hair. Their faces impish, their arms twisted around each other. Beneath them the caption:

JASON JUNIOR AND ALVIN—OUR FUTURE. Sad, the lives of folks, when their kids died before them.

Cathy must have missed her father. She never spoke of him. Yet Sarah had never seen her staring at his pictures in their New York apartment with as much intensity as she had shown looking at her grandfather.

On another panel there was a photograph of Mama Dear, young, tiny, beautiful, and black with thick coarse hair pulled back from her smiling face. Did smiles never change?

On the next panel were the photographs of Mrs. Johnson and her husband, Jason junior, on their wedding day, and one of Cathy, four months old, lying naked on a quilt, pushing herself up on strong dimpled arms.

A knock sounded on the door. Mother Dear opened it and came in. "Honey, tell me what I can do for you." The old woman came to stand beside her.

"Nothing," Sarah said. "I'm all right." Mama Dear searched through Sarah's eyes anxiously and Sarah hurried to assure her. "I'm okay. I'm getting used to being in here, with the pictures."

Mama Dear looked around at the old photographs and sighed. "They takes some getting used to," she said. "Look at that Prudence. A good woman. She'd been good long before the sixties when things in this country seemed to take a turn for the better. She was here, fighting for the rights of folks long before that. Prudence and Master Dixon was in the forefront of that fight.

"I been happy in this house, Sarah Richardson. Because in this house love flows. From the time we come, Master Dixon fixed it so that Big Red went into colleges and churches and meetings telling folks how blacks got beaten up and lynched and burned alive in the South. Big Red was always a man with courage, and when he come here and got to preaching, he got to sounding downright educated.

"Big Red never lied to them. He told them he was wanted in the South for killing a sheriff, for which he wasn't sorry. But he told them, 'When Brother Dixon opened up his home to me, I got to knowing that a thing such as brotherhood was possible. That got me to changing,' he said. 'Now, I'm warning y'all that I ain't fully changed. But I'm on my way. . . .' "

Looking at the photo of the boys with their arms around each other, she sighed. "We tried so hard to keep love strong in this house and on these acres," she said softly. "But then our boys went into the army. I don't know where they got the notion that the way to save democracy was to go into other folks' lands and kill 'em. We was all so upset. We known then that things had to change—and they sure did.

"Alvin, he was the first to go—in Korea. Then Prudence took to her bed—cancer, don't you know. After she died, Master Dixon commenced to dying too. Grieving, don't you know. He lost his appetite. They had worked together for so long, trying to make things right for folks. They talked at meetings, traveled together. And right here in this house, Prudence gave classes—in nursing, quilt making, helping to train folks from poorer countries. Soon after Prudence died poor Master Dixon took to his bed too.

"Jason took good care of him, they was that close. Jason used to tour the country telling about what happened in the South. He preached, gave speeches, made us a good living.

But he give up all that to care for Master Dixon. Oh, Big Red picked that man up like he was a baby, set him in the garden, bathed him, wiped his backsides.

"Awful to see a man will hisself to death—especially when he done so much good. Fighting in the courts against Jim Crow, against the wrongs done to Indians, foreigners. Then for him to will hisself to die . . ." She shook her head sadly. "Grieving will do that to you.

"He left Jason this house and the land. He ain't had no family, you see. Those few who outlived him was rich, and scattered thither and yon through the years."

Mama Dear's eyes moved from photograph to photograph. "Fifty years, and he ups and dies. Who'd think a big, evil man like Big Red would just up and die before me! His son—don't you see. His being so relieved that it was Alvin and not Li'l Jason dying over there made Big Red think he had sinned. Then Li'l Jason up and died. That caused a weakness of will. I seen it in his eyes, the same look in Master Dixon's.

"But he had me!" she cried in sudden rage. "He had me! I ain't never just gone off like Li'l Jason had! I lived beside him and in him—always!" Then the rage died, as sudden as it had come. In calm voice she resumed:

"So you see, my dear, everyone who had anything to do with this house left in it chunks of themselves. It's a house of ghosts." She chuckled mysteriously. "Good ones," she said. "You'll see, Sarah—you'll like them. They'll like you."

She went to the door, then turned back to say what she had come to say in the first place. "Sarah, don't you worry about Catherine's friends. They ain't bad kids. They just don't know yet what they got in they heads. Still, if you don't want to be troubled with them, Clarice'll take you where you want to go, or I'll get somebody to take you around. Lottie Richardson's li'l girl don't have to be beholden to no bits of fluff. No, sir. Not Lottie Richardson's girl."

Five

 A week had passed and Sarah still hadn't gone out with the gang and so had had no opportunity to try out her charm. The gang drove off mornings—Fred, Sheila, and Cathy in Milt's Porsche; Betty and Jody in Jody's Oldsmobile. Sarah had to depend on Mrs. Johnson to take long walks along the dunes, from where they looked out at fishing boats going out to sea. Some evenings they went down to watch fishermen unloading their catch and to buy fish and mussels and lobsters from them. Other days she helped Mama Dear in her garden—cleaning dead leaves from plants that grew in the sandy soil and helping cut long-stemmed roses, gladiolas, and lilies of the valley. Some were for the house; others she helped crate for Alicia to take to market.

"It doesn't make much," Mama Dear said. "Just something I love to do." Mrs. Johnson explained: "My father-in-law made a decent living with his speeches. Since he died, it's just make do."

Sarah missed playing the piano. How long could she fight against her daily habit of practice, against the urge to play—and chance having Mrs. Johnson and Mama Dear make her even more hated by their praise? More, she loathed tending flowers. The thought of the thorns of roses ripping her fingers and ruining her hands terrified her. She often thought of going home. But Mrs. Johnson, sensing her desperation, made arrangements for Sarah to go with the others.

Sarah drove in the back of Jody's old Oldsmobile to the beach, hoping that with them at least she might break through to some kind of communication, but Jody and Betty were in love. Sitting behind them, all Sarah could do was to stare at their heads touching and listen to their low tones, suggestively cooing. From the start, Sarah realized that the communal blanket Cathy provided for her friends was off limits to her. Instead she spread her beach towel near enough to bridge the distance between them, to hear what they were saying or to study them, unnoticed, behind her sunglasses, keeping alert for an opportunity to fit in.

Cathy and her friends had brought more clothes to the Cape than she. Every day each girl wore a different bikini. Sarah had brought only two. But she wore only the blue print. She would have preferred to wear the more expensive white-on-white. She liked it. It looked better on her, but she did not want to chance their probable black-on-black jokes. She hated being forced into playing Cathy's games. She hated it that Cathy's games affected her.

At one point, when she accidentally locked eyes with Sheila, quickly, before Sheila could look away, she spoke: "Sheila, about the brown-and-tan—"

Sheila widened her eyes and turned from her. Sarah's face burned. She went back to reading her book, *The Bluest Eye*, but found that she completed a chapter without having seen one word.

She looked at Fred often. He sat on the opposite side of the blanket. Always she found him looking away from her, out to sea. She felt his guilt. He had never allowed others to dictate his attitude. But since coming to the Cape, strangely, she had never once found herself in the same part of the room with him. And rarely did she get a chance to look into his eyes.

"You know," Sheila said, "I never want to go back to the city. If I had my druthers, I'd stay here—make living on the beach my life."

"In the sun?" Betty asked. "Like this? Life would soon become a bore, don't you think? I'm always glad to get away from studies. But I'm always anxious to get back. I'm so glad that I took architecture. I find it so exciting."

"The architecture course, or meeting me?" Jody joked. They laughed.

"Of course I'm joking," Sheila said. "Law is going to be my life. But I also love this. I want to live, to play, raise hell, before I settle down to marry."

"Marry?" Betty laughed. "I thought we were going to be career women. Love 'em and leave 'em, that sort of thing."

"How come you didn't tell me that before?" Jody said. "You waited until I fell, to tell me that you might leave me?"

"Don't you know a joke when you hear one?" Betty spoke in her most babyish voice.

"I haven't decided what I want," Cathy said. "My mother is always trying to make of me what she wants. She wanted me to be a pianist, then a violinist, then a dancer—you know, beautiful, graceful—the Swan Lake Princess. When all that failed, she left it up to me."

"So, what did you decide you wanted to be, princess?" Milt James asked.

"A rich wife," Cathy said.

"I'm at your service," Milt said.

"But, Cathy," Sheila said, "Milt's got such kinky hair. What if you should marry him and have a daughter with his kind of hair? You couldn't even comb it."

"I don't know," Cathy said. "Milt's hair's kinky, but his mother's white. I have good hair, so maybe our kid will not do too bad."

"Anyway, that leaves Fred out," Sheila said, looking over to Fred, flirting openly. "Fred, we probably would have curly-haired children if we decided to hitch up."

"But they might have coarse or nappy hair," Betty said. "Then what would you do?" Sarah wanted to talk, to ask them what was good hair? What was bad hair? She fought the urge to challenge them.

Fred rubbed his hands over his head. "Sheila, my children will always need their hair combed. Because my children will have hair as nappy as mine."

"With you, Fred, it wouldn't matter." Sheila kept her eyes looking into his, a smile hovering around her lips provocatively.

"Well, then"—Fred rubbed his hands together in pretended anticipation—"how long did you say before you finished school?"

"Not that long." Sheila kept looking over Cathy's head into his eyes. "Nothing takes forever. . . ."

"Not even your life," Cathy said in a tone that was blunt, threatening.

Sheila looked surprised. "Cathy, can't you take a joke?"

"Never at my expense," Cathy said, then stood up. "God, it's hot. Let's do what we came to do." She ran to the water. The others all followed.

Sarah watched them go, wild, free—certain in their concept of themselves. She closed her eyes. What the hell did they know about charm? What did Sheila know? And why had she asked Sheila about the brown-and-tan room? Had she actually intended to apologize? What for? For having been invited to stay in the grandest room ever? A flush of embarrassment forced sweat to push out of her pores.

"Hiya, what are you reading?" Sarah looked up to find Alicia standing over her. She handed her the book *The Bluest Eye* by Toni Morrison. Hear of it?"

"Nope, never have," Alicia said, flipping through its pages.

"Great book—an American classic. This is my third time reading it."

"If it's that good I'd like to read it. May I borrow it?"

"Sure, soon's I'm finished."

"Enjoying yourself up here?" Alicia handed her back the book.

"Sort of," Sarah lied. She wanted to say she was having

an absolutely miserable time, had been since the first day she had come. "Will you join me?" She moved to make room on the towel for Alicia to sit.

"I'm meeting friends." Alicia looked around. "I want to get in some swimming before I head for the house." She looked out at the water. "The others seem to be having great fun. Why don't you go in?"

Sarah looked out to see Cathy and her friends laughing, climbing on each other's backs, diving into the water, disappearing beneath its surface, then reappearing. The world certainly belonged to them.

"I can't swim," Sarah said. "I have only been to the beach twice in my entire life."

Always disciplined and close to her music, somehow she had never felt this need to swim. But now a deep yearning took possession of her. Swimming had become suddenly essential to her life.

"I would teach you—but I don't intrude on Cathy's friends. Are you afraid of water?"

"I don't think so."

"Those who are can end up drowning their teacher."

"If you promise to teach me, I'll not be difficult. I know everything that I'm not supposed to do." How sinister, Cathy's authority reaching this girl who only worked for her grandmother.

"I don't know," Alicia said. "Here come your friends." Sarah saw they were coming back. "And here come mine," Alicia said. "See you back at the house."

Alicia ran off to meet her friends—two girls, as tall and long legged as she. They ran together to the water, dived in.

She could see them swimming away from the shore. In minutes they were like moving sticks—arms and legs taking them out into the distance.

The brief encounter with Alicia made Sarah realize how much she had been missing the simple act of opening and closing her mouth. Talking had loosened her tension and she stretched out, finally relaxed. The group walked up and threw themselves down on the blanket. All except Milt. He walked over to Sarah. "Look, girl," he said. "We're letting you spread out next to us. But not if all you can do is talk to servants."

Water from his wet body dripped down on her and Sarah could only stare at him, gaping. Fred spoke from the other side of the blanket. "Hey, watch that, man. Don't be talking to Sarah like that. And what's this putting down Grandmother's girl?"

"I agree with Milt," Sheila said in her most arrogant tone. "Do we have to bring ourselves down to the level of servants just because they happen to be white?"

Sarah waited for Cathy to come to Alicia's defense. She had known the girl most of her life. But Cathy ignored them. Stretched out on the blanket, leaning back to catch the full glare of the sun, lips curled up in a satisfied smirk, she said, "Before I leave this summer I intend to be as black as Sarah." A hush fell—took them off the subject of Alicia.

"I'll settle for being as brown as Betty," Sheila broke the short silence. She laughed. "Brown Betty—get it?"

"Never happen," Betty said. "I'm golden. The golden girl. That special color that those of your complexion can't find in a bottle."

Sarah felt her scalp tingle. Milt had insulted her. He had slurred Alicia. Yet these intelligent, well-educated, knowledgeable people limited their conversation to complexion and hair texture as though indeed they lived in outer space. Was this what Cathy had given up her friendship for? For these shallow people she had labored to acquire charm?

Fred grabbed a handful of sand. Standing over Cathy, he poured it slowly on her stomach. Cathy's eyes remained closed, her head back, a slow, sensuous smile curving her lips. Desire flamed in Fred's eyes. He picked up another handful.

Angered, Milt walked away from Sarah. He went to sit next to Cathy on the blanket and leaned against her raised knee. Fred kept pouring sand on Cathy's stomach—slowly, slowly. . . .

Even with her eyes closed Cathy gave off an aura of controlled wickedness. Her gold pubic hairs escaped her black bikini around the legs. They glowed against her thigh. Passion inflamed Fred. He kept pouring sand on the flat stomach.

The lewdness of it. The excitement of it. A wave of restlessness rushed through Sarah, tormenting her. She felt the waste of her unnoticed shapely limbs, her smooth silky black skin. She gazed over to Fred. For one startled moment their eyes locked. He saw the appeal in hers. Quickly he turned from her, grabbed Cathy's arm, pulled her to her feet. "Come on, let's get this crap washed off," he said.

They walked away, Cathy and Fred. Sarah watched them —the two whom she wanted most to be with. She watched them stop at the water's edge, standing so close, the water framed them like a picture.

"Come on, Sheila"—Milt nudged Sheila with his foot— "let's take another dip."

"Sorry, Milt. I want to catch up on my rest." Sheila didn't like Milt. She did think like him on issues concerning class, but she tolerated him only because he happened to be Cathy's friend.

"What did we come all the way up here for, if it's to lie around sleeping?" Milt growled. "I might as well have stayed in the city."

"You didn't come up here to go dipping with me," Sheila reminded him. "Whatever the reason you did come, I came to rest." She turned on her stomach, and laid her head on her arm. Milt reached down, took her arm, yanked her to her feet, and dragged her struggling toward the water, to where Cathy and Fred were standing.

Betty and Jody lay on their stomachs, their eyes closed. Were they sleeping or did they just not want to become involved? Sarah sighed, opened her book, and began to read. She must have fallen asleep, because some time later the sounds of their voices awakened her. They were all together on their blanket.

"Why won't you be a doctor like your dad, Fred?" she heard Betty say.

"Naw, that takes too many years," Fred answered. "Basketball is the quickest way to fame—and that's what I know to do. I've been playing all my life."

"But what if something happens?" Betty insisted.

"Like what?"

"Like to your knees, your elbows, or your ankles. You hear about that sort of thing happening to athletes all the time."

"I'll wait till that happens." Fred shrugged. "Then maybe I'll think of medicine."

"Hardly a grand gesture," Betty said in a way of a challenge. "I'd think you'd take medicine as a way to help the poor. We have too few doctors."

"My God, Betty." Cathy laughed. "Since when the concern about the poor? You haven't decided to go in for charity work, have you? I'm with Fred. Take those millions and run."

"Stop being glib," Betty said. "Fred's father had to work hard to become a doctor. Fred's got to be proud. It seems that instead of getting more black doctors, the doors are closing for opportunities. Those of us who can—"

"Right, right." Fred put up his hands as though to fend her off. "My old man didn't finish medical school until I was twelve. Then he had to do his residencies. Man, we were always needing. Always on the verge of poverty. I don't have that kind of time."

"But there's something to be said about keeping in your parents' footsteps," Jody McCoy finally spoke, his soft voice commanding attention. "My dad's convinced me of that. Dad believes in old money. The only way to have old money is to build a structure. A class structure. *That* we don't have. He's an architect, his father was an architect, my older brother is an architect, and that's what I intend to be. We're all working together. That's the only way to build a firm foundation, which eventually can carry the weight of an entire people."

"Milt," Sheila said, "what about you? Are you going into boxing or prizefighting like your old man? That ought to help build your biceps. That way you can try dragging men around for a change."

Sarah sat up to see how Milt would react. Milt's face, already reddened by sun, turned a brighter red. His eyes jerked around their watery sockets.

"But Milt's already rich," Cathy said, coming to his rescue. "Milt doesn't have a thing to do in this life. His father's in real estate, and his parents put most of their money in trust for him. Isn't that wild? All he has to do when his folks are gone is to lie back and spend. He can live a life spaced out between earth and sky. That's the kind of living I want."

"Cathy, I don't believe you." Sarah surprised herself defending her friend from her own words. "You know there's more to life than being useless."

Milt's fury had been building; now it found its mark. "What do you know about anything," he shouted at Sarah, "you with an uncle who's a janitor and a mother who scrubs floors to make a living? Isn't that so, Cathy? Isn't that what you told me—"

"Then she told you a lie!" Sarah shouted back. Anger forced her to her feet and she stood glaring at them, waiting to take on any one of them. "My uncle may be a janitor, but my mother never in her life scrubbed floors! Do you hear that? Never in her entire life."

Six

Sweat pushed through Sarah's pores, rolled down the sides of her face and neck, and soaked her bikini, making it cling to her. Then it slid down her thighs and her calves into her sandals. Walking, walking, her mind blank—except she still heard shrill laughter. Still glimpsed bare backs turned to her. That came in flashes, then once again blankness and the jarring anger.

"My uncle may be a janitor, but my mother never in her life scrubbed floors. . . ." Words? Her words? Had they been used by her? Walking, walking, her feet leading her, then once again blankness. Willful blankness. "My mother never scrubbed floors." She stopped walking and covered her face with both hands to hold back tears. Yet they came. Big tears. Hot tears, welling from her depths, flowing through her eyes, down her cheeks into her mouth. Salty,

salty tears. Her words turned to salt. She had sinned! She had turned in against herself. What lures had they offered to have pulled her down? Was it possible that deep inside she had the desire to be like them?

No! Never! Still she had come out to seduce them. Instead they had ensnared her.

No, Lottie Richardson had never scrubbed floors. Her Aunt Gladys had. Aunt Gladys had taken care of Lottie and of Lottie's child. Aunt Gladys still scrubbed floors. "And I love her, love her, love her . . ."

Sarah's feet had led her to the old house. Almost there, she saw Mama Dear on the front porch rocking. Sarah walked up the steps and attempted to walk by. But Mama Dear caught her hand. "Back so soon?" she asked. "Where're the others?"

"Down at the beach." Sarah kept her head turned, not wanting the woman to see her tears. She tried to pull her hand away. But the strong old hands held on. "What's the matter, honey?"

"Nothing. I—I'm going home."

"Going home? You'll do no such a thing."

"Please. Please. Mama Dear, I'm going to take a train. Will you call me a taxi?"

"I'll do no such a thing, 'less you tell me what done happened," Mama Dear said.

"Nothing." Sarah shook her head. "I—I just want to go home. I—I'm homesick."

"Homesick, is it? Poor dear. Now—I ought to have thought about that. Your first trip away, ain't it? Folks sometimes misses where they come from like that. When I got here I was homesick. Yet you got to know Mississippi was the last place I wanted to get back to.

"Yes, suh, ought to have thought that one out. But, Sarah, I promise I'll do better. . . ."

"It's not you," Sarah cried. "Please, it's not you. . . ."

Fat tears flowed freely, her nostrils stopped up. She breathed through her mouth.

"Dear, dear . . . oh, my dear. I'm so sorry. . . ." Mama Dear's hand fluttered helplessly before the volume of tears. She played with the ruffles at her neck. "We . . . kind a forced you to go off with them—didn't we, now? I ought to have known better. You and they . . . different. But I sure don't want you to go, on account of them, you and your pretty face—and I sure wants to get to know you better."

The old woman's sincerity only made the tears flow harder. How could she tell such a good woman that her tears had nothing to do with the others, and everything to do with the shock of finding out she had more of them in her than she had admitted?

"What's all the commotion?" Mrs. Johnson had come to the door. "My God, Sarah, what's happened?"

"Sarah's talking about leaving us, Clarice. She wants to take the train back to the city. Must have been something that happened down at the beach."

"What could have happened to make you cry this way, Sarah? Did someone say something to you? Did Cathy? Did that awful boy Milt?"

Sarah shook her head, kept shaking her head. She knew that others might put the blame on Milt. Milt had caused her anger, not her tears. How could she explain that to Mrs. Johnson, or to anyone?

"I have to go, that's all," Sarah said, feeling the approach of hysteria. "They didn't want me to come. I had no right to come." But if she hadn't come, she might never have seen so deeply inside herself.

"I wanted you to come, Sarah. I want you to stay. Don't I count? Am I too old?" Mrs. Johnson tried to turn her misery into a joke. It didn't work. Sarah shook her head.

"I want to go home," she said.

"Okay, if that's what you want," Mrs. Johnson said. "But first I think you ought to rest. It's not good to stay so long in the sun, then to get this upset. Lottie will have my head if you go home sick."

Mrs. Johnson led Sarah up the stairs and into the room. She helped her take off her bikini, forced her to lie down, pulled the covers over her, and brushed back her hair. "There, there, lie still. Think things over. I'll be going home soon. You can leave when I go. I—Mother will look out for you. Don't answer now. Rest. We'll talk when you get up."

Sarah watched Mrs. Johnson walk to the door. She had thought to get up after the woman left, pack her things, then leave the house to find a way to the station. Instead she lay staring at the closed door, too exhausted from crying to move. She thought of Uncle Sam, remembering the day when she had lost her keys from around her neck, and had no car fare, and had set out on the two-mile hike to his house. It had been the coldest day of the year, with the temperature reaching below zero.

On the way her hands and feet had frozen. They had

become like blocks of ice. Each step she took had been a nightmare. Tears had frozen on her cheeks. Snot had run from her nose and that, too, had frozen. She had wanted to stand still and die. Instead, she had inched on until she had come to the basement apartment. Without her having to ring the bell the door opened. There stood her uncle Sam— big, broad, and handsome.

He had scooped her up in his great arms, had taken her into the bathroom, had stripped off her clothes, bathed her in ice-cold water, dried her in a big towel, rubbed her until her blood flowed again and her body tingled. Wrapping her in a blanket he sat with her in his arms next to a radiator, had cradled her, while looking at television, until Aunt Gladys had come home. Her mother had called them to alert them Sarah was missing. But she had spent that night sleeping between her aunt and uncle, feeling so loved—so protected.

Sarah awakened as the setting sun sent its fading glow through the trees, reflecting the leaves shimmering like filigree over the polished floor. She lay staring out at the silent pictures on the walls. They stared back. She had gone to sleep wanting to go home. Now opening her eyes in the grand room forced her to marvel at Mama Dear who, seeing her for the first time, had entrusted to her the guardianship of her ghosts.

The room pleased her, the honor flattered her and acted as balm to her bruised spirit. She wanted to stay. Better to awaken in this privacy than at home, where her brooding hen of a mother waited with her I-told-you-so stare.

A knocking on the terrace roused her. The lone branch of

the tree beat against the terrace rail. A blue bird perched on the branch, turned its head first one way then another to better stare at her out of a bead of an eye. Getting out of bed, Sarah went out on the terrace. "Oochie koochie coo," she sang to the bird. The eye of the astonished bird flashed with indignation. It flew away. Sarah laughed, then shivered with delight as, for the first time in her life, a breeze played over her fully naked body.

A knock sounded at the door. Sarah dashed back into the room and dived beneath the bedcovers before calling, "Come in."

Mrs. Johnson pushed her head into the room. "You awake, Sarah?" She came into the room and over to the bed. "Feel better?"

"Yes—much."

"Good. Then why don't you get dressed and come down-stairs? Mother's friends have arrived and we're about to sit down to dinner." Annoyance at having to sit with Cathy or her friends showed in her face, and Mrs. Johnson said, "Sarah, don't let those flighty friends of Cathy's spoil your time here. God knows you work hard enough during the school year. You deserve a break. Lottie won't let you rest if you're home. She actually believes that everybody is as strong and undauntable as she. She can't conceive that we ordinary folks got limits." She paused to search Sarah's face, then she added, "I want you to stay on here for a while— even after I leave. I want you to get to know Mother better. You'll see, things'll get better."

"Mrs. Johnson, about today, about Cathy and her friends.

They are like they are. I guess when I came I thought that it made no difference. It did. I don't belong."

"In this house everybody belongs," Mrs. Johnson stopped her. "Can you say a fool thing like that, after you have met my mother-in-law? After you have been in her haven?" That's not what Sarah had started to say. Nevertheless, she let Mrs. Johnson go on. "There are no barriers in here, not between young people—certainly not with people she likes. And she likes you, Sarah."

Sarah looked up into the sooty blue eyes and smiled. It grieved her that Mrs. Johnson and her mother were no longer close. Those years when they had been friends had been the best years of her life. She remembered the women laughing, scheming on how to "put one over" on the establishment. The one time they had failed, so had their friendship. Sarah understood both women. To her, in that failure there had been no right, no wrong. But one didn't discuss that with Lottie. Sighing, Sarah said, "I like Mama Dear too —Mrs. Johnson, I don't want to go home. I want to stay."

"Great. I'm glad. So get on up and come on down." She pulled the covers from the bed. Sarah sat up. "Thank you, Mrs. Johnson. Thanks for—this break." Mrs. Johnson winked at her and went out.

Seven

 "Enfin, mes amis. It's too hard to be true. I wanted so much to come in May, then in June —and so now July. Still, *Dieu merci,* I am here. It's that son of mine. Impossible. Work, work, work—that's his life. What is a poor mother to do?"

Voluptuous. Madame Armand, stretched out on the sofa fanning herself with an oversized silver-and-black fan, had to be the most sensuous woman ever. Big breasted, tall with rounded arms—their small, handy pouches of fat pushing out at the back of her sleeveless dress. Beautiful. Dark reddish-brown, a long thin nose, her wide brown eyes decorated by heavy eyebrows and lush lashes. Her long hair made unruly by small waves was relentlessly pulled back into a ponytail that emphasized her beautiful profile. Big, feminine, dainty despite sweat pouring down the sides of her face that kept one hand busy wiping.

"You ought to have come here right from Martinique and waited here for the boy," Mrs. Johnson said.

"No, no. That I did not want. The minute I hear he's in Paris, I fly there. That way, I know I must see him—the first time in five years. So I go with him to Washington, to New York, *et voilà*—here I am."

"It's been so many years, so many years." Mama Dear rocked her rocker, sighing. "So much has happened since we first met. Years of sadness, and of happiness, but so many of sadness." She rocked as she looked back in time, her face soft from memories.

"Mais oui," Madame Armand said. "Many years of happiness—true. The last time I came was for the interment of Big Red, *n'est-ce pas*?"

Cathy's friends sat on the sofa opposite the one on which she sat staring. Sarah too. She sat on the piano stool and couldn't look away from the lovely Madame Armand. "They used to call him that—Big Red, Big Jason, or big man. Oh, but they were happy, little Mama and her big man."

"The time before, you had come to help out at Li'l Jason's burial," Mama Dear reminded her.

"Quelle tristesse—so sad. . . ." Madame Armand looked at Mrs. Johnson, projecting sympathy. "Your father, he was so handsome," she said to Cathy.

"They died too young—both of them, Li'l Jason and Alvin," Mama Dear cried. "Alvin in Korea, Jason, he come back, met Clarice in New York, then he moved there. But they got married right here in this house. Catherine, she got baptized here. . . . Li'l Jason—what's so young a man doing passing from a stroke?" Her voice faltered. "I never known why He saved me," Mama Dear opened her hands and studied them. "I'd as soon have exchanged places with him—with Big Red. . . ."

"Mais, that's not for you to say." Madame Armand's tone turned teasing. "And who would I have to greet me, Mama Dear? If not you, nobody. The way I love this place?" She gazed around the cherished room. *"Non, non,* he can take anybody He want, but never Chère Mama."

Her banter, her lilting voice, chased away the sadness. The faces of her young audience relaxed into smiles. "You see, Madame Dixon—Prudence—she come to my home in Martinique when I am so unhappy. My lover had say to me he can never marry me. So I take the poison. I am going to die when Prudence come and knock on the door. She sit by my bed and take care of me. She save my life—and then she bring me back with her—to this house."

"Good things always happen in this house," Mama Dear said from her creaking rocking chair. "Best proof is me and Big Red. Guess in twenty, thirty, forty years—bad as well as good's bound to happen."

"But so much good did happen, Chère Mama," Madame Armand said. "The good is more than the bad. Remember Hega, the girl from India," Madame Armand said joining in reminiscence. "She was here with Amina, from the Gold Coast. Two lovely girls—before their time, *n'est-ce pas*? They leave their homes and come here, by some strange ways. But what they wanted was to nurse. And we—Mama Dear, Prudence, and me—we make this and that and we give parties—to raise money. We sent them to college, then we helped them to go back home. They were both head nurses.

"Mais, Clarice," Madame Armand observed, now changing the drift of the conversation, "you are still so young, so chic. And me—like a cow."

Not a cow. Definitely not a cow. Simply beautiful, with her skin stretched to unbelievable smoothness over her plump body. She looked younger than Mrs. Johnson, except that one kept remembering her hardworking son. "You are right. You must stay slim—and young. Life is so short, *n'est-ce pas*? That's what I tell my Jean Pierre. Too short to leave his mother and just go. But what to do? He cannot live on the same little island with his father. So he leave Martinique and go to Africa. Africa! Do you know how far is Africa from Martinique!"

Her roving eyes settled on Sarah at the piano, and in her delightful way of jumping from one subject to another she cried, "But you—I did not meet you. What is your name?"

"Sarah."

"Oh la la, Sarah, *quel joli nom*—a pretty name for a pretty girl, *n'est-ce pas*?" Madame Armand exposed perfect teeth in a broad smile. "Mama Dear, what lovely children. You are like dear Prudence—bringing all such lovely-looking people together in this wonderful house. Sometimes, you know, I feel so sorry that I go back to Martinique—and that man!" She shrugged. "He didn't give to me his name, but he give to me Jean Pierre. When I come back to this house again, Jean Pierre, he is six—seven. . . ." She looked over to the couch, at Fred. "I meet you?"

"Yes—I'm Fred—Fred Hamilton."

"Ahh, Fred," she said, shaking out her sodden handkerchief. "This is so—so *mouillé*. I want another. Can I make you to get my *petit sac*—my little purse—from the dining room?" Eagerly Fred jumped to his feet. He rushed stumbling into the dining room. In one second he had come back with the purse. "Such a sweet boy. And so handsome." She lifted plush eyelashes and lowered them. *"Quel charme,"* she murmured, watching him as he stumbled back to the couch.

She moved around with the agility of a much thinner woman, making room on the couch. "Come, Clarice, sit, tell me what you do since I did not see you." Mrs. Johnson walked over to sit beside her and she asked, "Clarice, you must tell me how you keep so young."

"By trying," came Mrs. Johnson's dry reply. "It ain't easy."

Hearing the sound of glass against glass in the dining room as Alicia set the table, Mama Dear stood up and walked to the door. In the doorway she stopped to ask Madame Armand, "How is Jean Pierre's father these days?"

Madame Armand shrugged. "Old and getting older—and evil. He make too much money. Still buying land and when Jean Pierre come home, he tracks him down to fight. He want to disown Jean Pierre. But what to do. That is his only son."

"What's there to fight about?" Mama Dear asked.

"Tout," Madame Armand said. "Everything. Money, politic. The old man he love Martinique like it is. Jean Pierre? He want things changed. A free Martinique, he say. He want to change his father. But his father, he is rich. He make so

much money on that island, with his sugar, his coffee. He is old. He must not be old and poor too." She shook her head. "They cannot talk. What to do? They're men. . . ."

"And a mighty fine young man he is, your Jean Pierre," Mama Dear said. "If he hadn't come through that door with you, I'd have sworn that wasn't the same boy who come to Li'l Jason's funeral."

Madame Armand said, "He was a boy, now he is a man."

At that Mama Dear stood and went into the dining room, where they heard her say, "Oh, so you heard, did you? Now, I ain't told no lie. You sure 'nough turned out to be one fine-looking man. Wish to God Mrs. Dixon was here to see you. She sure would have been proud."

The deep-throated murmur and the hearty laughter forced every eye to the doorway. Even the men were waiting to see the son of this fabulous woman. Then there he stood, in the doorway, leaning against the frame looking at them.

He was his mother's child, judging from his dark good looks. His skin was darker—darkened by many suns, reddened by many winds. He wore a thick mustache, which gave his face a look of extreme strength. Relaxed in his tan silk shirt and linen slacks, with his thick, curly hair, and his feet pushed into loafers, he looked more like an idle rich man than the hardheaded revolutionary described by his mother.

"C'est Madame Johnson, n'est-ce pas?" he said, going over to the couch.

"Oui." Madame Armand nodded. "You see, Clarice? My son, he remember."

"He certainly did get to be a handsome young man." Mrs. Johnson smiled up at him. "And he remembers me."

"But you are the same," Madame Armand said. "And my son, he never forget a voice, a poem, or somebody's mistake." Pointing to Cathy, she said. *"C'est sa fille*—her daughter."

Jean Pierre turned and, seeing Cathy, laughed. *"Mais elle n'est plus bébé."*

"He said you are no longer a baby," Madame Armand translated.

"Elle est belle." The look in his eyes spoke of his admiration.

And Cathy cried out, "Don't translate. I know you have just made my day."

"Pardon . . ." He didn't understand. No one offered an explanation. All were impressed by the young man, his bearing—broad, tall, and older than the other men in the room. He had diminished them with his presence.

Sheila stretched her six feet up from the couch and held out her hand. "I'm Cathy's friend, Sheila. I am so glad that you're here." She smiled seductively into his eyes.

Jean Pierre smiled back. He waited for her to sit down before turning his smile on Betty. Betty deepened her dimples and widened her golden eyes in total admiration. "I'm Betty," she said, offering a limp hand. He bowed over it, then moved on. He offered his hand to Milt. Milt hesitated. Fear hovered in his watery blue eyes. He sensed an adversary in this stranger standing over him—as dark as his father and more handsome. The hand stayed out until he accepted it.

"Milt, Milton James."

Jody jumped to his feet and pushed an enthusiastic hand out, then pumped Pierre's hand hard. "Jody McCoy. Glad to have this chance to meet a true Martinican—and your mother."

"Hey, watch that. We don't play that around here," Fred joked. They all laughed. That put them at ease. But Cathy preferred tension to ease. Standing and stepping up to him, she used a husky voice: "Jean Pierre? That name's so . . . French. Things were getting boring around here. Now that we have a man in the crowd, things ought to get interesting."

Jean Pierre stepped back to put distance between them. *"Pardon? Je ne comprends pas.* Maybe if you please speak more slowly."

Madame Armand came to his rescue. "Jean Pierre doesn't understand English when he's too tired. But he must learn to. He has too much business here."

"Elle dit bienvenu." Sarah amazed herself by her audacity and her knowledge of French, for she rarely spoke it outside of school.

"Mais vous parlez français très bien, mademoiselle," he said.

"Un peu," she said, her heart pounding against her chest as in fear. Yet she felt a fierce satisfaction. She knew that all eyes had turned to look at her.

"Où avez-vous appris votre français?" Jean Pierre came to stand beside the piano.

"À l'école," Sarah said.

"Mes félicitations, ma belle," Madame Armand said. Then

to Jean Pierre, "You see, my son, things will not be so dull for you here, *n'est-ce pas?*"

"Well," Sheila snorted, turning her aristocratic head from them. "Our little Sarah has at least one saving grace. She speaks French."

"Whatever do you mean?" Mrs. Johnson retorted in her blunt, straightforward manner. "Sarah happens to be a most intelligent girl." Then to Mrs. Armand: "Sarah hasn't been feeling too well. She's been talking of leaving us—of going home."

"But of course she cannot go," the impetuous Madame Armand said. "Who then will interpret for my Jean Pierre when he is too tired? *La fatigue,* you know," she said, confiding to Sarah.

At that moment Alicia came to the door; dinner was being served.

They ate silently for the most part, except for Madame Armand's constant complaints.

"I tell you, Clarice, what is a mama to do? My Jean Pierre, he's so far away from me. What if something happens to him? What will I do? All he thinks is—*comment se dit sylviculture,*" she said.

"Forestry," Sarah answered.

"Oui. Il est fou de ça."

They were silent again, then Jean Pierre said to Sarah, *"Faîtes savoir à Chère Mama que sa cuisine est, comme toujours, formidable."*

"Mama Dear," Sarah said to the old woman as she came

to sit at the head of the table, "Jean Pierre wants you to know that your cooking is, as usual, fantastic."

"You remember?" Mama Dear said. "How nice that you remember."

"My son, he never forgets," Madame Armand said, and Milt looked across the table at Sarah.

"Sarah, I must say the New York City educational system has done all right by you."

Surprised, Sarah looked across at Milt. Their eyes met, and realizing that he hadn't meant it as a compliment, she turned away quickly.

Cathy laughed. "Yeah—all Sarah needs now is a bit of grooming. Never can tell. She might make it—yet."

"A little grooming and staying out of the sun," Milt said, chuckling. "One shade darker and we won't even be able to see if she makes it."

"Oh, come on," Sheila chimed in. "She can't stay out of the sun forever. Even moles must come out for vitamin D."

Madame Armand looked up, with a deep frown pleating her brow. She looked first at Milt, then at Sheila. "My ears, they do not hear this," she said. "In this house we know only love. How you talk to your friend so—before strangers? How you talk things about blackness. You do not like us— *que c'est malheureux*—because we are black? Or did you want to make this pretty Sarah feel ugly? You are not kind."

"Milt didn't mean it the way it sounded," Cathy said, turning angry eyes to Milt. But Mrs. Johnson's anger eclipsed all others.

"How dare you sit at this table in my mother-in-law's house and expose your limitations?" Her eyes blazed. "By trying to insult Sarah you have insulted us all."

"It's time for dessert," Mama Dear said primly. Getting up, she walked from the table, her slight body stiff. They followed her movements with their eyes until she had pushed through the swinging door.

By the time they had finished dessert, the atmosphere at the table had become too heavy. Betty, attempting to change the mood, looked over to Jean Pierre. "I never knew anyone by the name of Jean Pierre before," she said. "But then I have never met a Frenchman before."

"Then, mademoiselle," Jean Pierre replied, "you know no Frenchman. I am not French. I am African—African-Caribbean, from Martinique to be precise. I do not live in France—nor do I have that desire."

The earlier incident had obviously forced him to a better command of the language. His answer plunged them in deeper discomfort.

All except Sarah. She had an irresistible urge to laugh. For some reason she felt free of restrictions, of the gloom that had been woven around her. She looked across the table into Cathy's narrowed eyes. Whatever plan Cathy might devise to get even, she didn't care.

With a carefree movement she rose from the table and, going to the parlor, sat at the piano and started to play. Yes, her uncle Sam worked as a janitor, her aunt Gladys scrubbed floors, and, goddamn, she played the hell out of the piano, and yes, she held her own in French.

"Look away, far away,
All ye folks that roam.
Look away, far away,
Far away from home . . .

Mrs. Johnson came to stand by the piano and join her in song.

"O'er land, o'er sea,
Rolling with a song,
Every sigh, every breeze,
Rolling you along . . ."

Mrs. Johnson's singing brought Sarah back to the time when their families had been close. When they had lived in the same building and Uncle Sam and Aunt Gladys had come bringing them fried chicken and biscuits and home-made cakes on Thursday evenings. There had been no talk about who worked where, or why they lived there. Everyone had enjoyed being with everybody else.

When had their differences started? When Cathy had changed schools and started going to Banning? When they had moved away? Sad—sad that so much had changed, and she had no answers. That no one seemed to have real answers.

"Bravo! Bravo!" Sarah turned to the sound of applause. Mrs. Johnson bowed, laughing. A lightness of spirit had taken over. "Mam'selle, but you have a grand talent," Jean Pierre said, laughing. He had enjoyed the song.

"Oui, so much talent. You are such a delight," Madame Armand said.

"Beautiful, beautiful." Mama Dear beamed. "Clarice kept saying you played well. I'm glad you finally give me the honor of hearing you." All the praise that she had known would be given to her, they gave. She began to play a Chopin polonaise, hoping that if her playing made a difference to the others, it would be a good difference.

"Gosh, Sarah, I didn't know you played." Fred came to stand beside Jean Pierre.

"Fred, I've been playing most of my life," Sarah said.

"No kidding? You are really something," he said in admiration. "First you come out talking all this French. Now I'm hearing you play the piano. Girl, you got talent you ain't even used."

"What do you know about me, Fred?"

"Guess I don't know much at that," he said. "When we get back to the city I'll drop around so you can fill me in."

But she knew all about him. She had known all about him and she had liked him—yesterday. But now? He did look so young, so insignificant today. Perhaps because of his silence on the beach? They had shamed her—no, she had shamed herself. Whatever, she remembered the time when his father swept the cafeteria in their grammar school. His father had been going to medical school then. His father had kept the cafeteria clean and she had fought Fred's battles. Yet when she had needed him he hadn't come to her defense.

"Do you play the jazz?" Jean Pierre asked. "I want that you play for me the jazz."

Sarah switched to playing her uncle's favorite, "Sophisticated Lady."

"Ahhh, Duke Ellington," Jean Pierre said in appreciation, snapping his fingers in time. The rest joined in, and they stamped their feet and hummed along.

"Congrats," Betty said from the doorway. "I am surprised. Pleasantly, I must say. I didn't know you played. No one ever told me."

Sarah refused to comment. Of course Betty knew. They all knew. They had seen the baby grand piano at her house when they came to wait for Cathy.

The others moved to the foyer, ready to leave for the night. But Cathy came back into the parlor. Going up to Jean Pierre she stood close enough so that their thighs touched. "Jean Pierre"—she gazed into his eyes—"you are coming with us, aren't you?"

"I regret, Cathy. I want so much to hear Sarah play the jazz." His eyes still gleamed in admiration of her, and he did appear to be affected by their touching thighs.

"You can always hear Sarah." Cathy moved closer. "That's all she ever does—hang around with the old and aging and play the piano. We young ones like to have a little time on the town."

"Another time, *chère* Cathy." Jean Pierre exchanged flirting glances with her. *"Mais,* it is the fatigue—*n'est-ce pas*? I prefer to stay tonight in this magnificent house and listen to beautiful music—and rest."

Cathy turned to Sarah. "Sarah, you always manage to make a spectacle of yourself. Pray this floor show won't cost you dear. . . . Coming, Fred?"

Fred followed Cathy out into the foyer but stuck his head back into the room to say, "Don't pay Cathy any mind, Sarah. You know how she is?"

The trouble was she did know how Cathy was. From the door she heard Sheila's mocking voice. "Cathy, what happened? You said that Jean Pierre was coming."

"That old man?" Cathy scoffed. "Dragging old folks around is just the same as having no one. That guy's got to be at least thirty."

"Who are you kidding?" Sheila's mockery had deepened. "Since when's a guy's age been a problem to you, Cathy?"

Laughter. The door slammed shut. Laughing at Cathy? They ought never to laugh at Cathy.

Eight

 Sarah listened as their laughter faded and waited for the desolation that usually came over her after they left without her. The dimming of lights, the emptiness, knowing that she had been left out once again. It didn't happen.

"You're not stopping, are you?" Mama Dear asked. She sat in her rocker, and its creaking filled the silence. "It's been so long since I heard such playing in this house."

"The piano has such a rich tone," Sarah said. "Somebody plays—do you?"

"No, my dear," Mama Dear said. "I keeps it tuned. Prudence, you know—she played. Kept this place alive with music. Hearing you—stirred up her spirit. Does her heart good."

Mama Dear guarded her ghosts. Looking at her, rocking, smiling, listening, Sarah almost felt them around her.

"Hear them moving," Mama Dear said. "They're out now —all of 'em. Sitting right out there on the steps, just a-listening. Claudine, don't it sound like old times?"

"Oui," Madame Armand answered. "It is so—so fine. Your music. It makes them come out to hear. Madame Dixon—she played fine, fine music too."

"I remember too," Jean Pierre said, joining in with the ghostly story. "This house—with all its goodness, its greatness, how happy it used to make me to be here, in this room, listening to Madame. . . .

"Alvin and Jason, the big brothers which I never had, were so kind. We used to sit outside of this door on the steps listening, listening. Chère Mama, I seem to remember —didn't you play?"

"Nooo, honey, not me. When life's been as miserable as mine was, it takes some doing to believe that you can do things normal folks do—even given a chance. My life been spent hiding, running. When I got here I was safe. Never gave a thought to something so trifling as a piano. Playing? Me?" She shook her head.

Sarah understood. Mama Dear thought the way Uncle Sam and Aunt Gladys did. The miracle of piano playing belonged to another generation or to geniuses—the jazz musicians. They had worked so hard that their happiness lay in thinking their "Puddin' " was a genius.

"Funny how life changes," Mama Dear said. "We ain't never had no television in this house. Only radio. But that was enough for Alvin and Jason to break up the closeness that we had to go off to war. Police action they called it.

Going off to other folks' land to kill 'em, leaving this house so big, so empty.

"Prudence, though, she never stopped playing. She filled the house up with sound—even after she got so sick. Sarah, she's happy Clarice brought you. This house been missing somebody like you." Mama Dear twisted her head as though waiting for a sound of agreement. She seemed to be welcoming the movement of someone on the stairs. A ghost? Ghosts? Sarah stared at the doorway, her eyes wide, expectant. And as she waited she heard the shouts of children, running, laughing up and down the steps, but no one appeared. Still, Mama Dear kept looking, listening, smiling.

"You are sad."

Sarah looked up into Jean Pierre's eyes. A thrill raced through her. She realized that he had spoken and was awaiting an answer. Then she heard him. "Sad?" she asked. "No, I'm not sad."

"Your friends—are you unhappy you did not go with them?"

"No, no. I wanted to be here—in this house," Sarah answered.

"They were not nice," he persisted. "They did not ask you."

"You mustn't take those kids seriously, Jean Pierre," Mrs. Johnson cautioned. "They're not half as bad as they sound."

"*Chère* Madame Johnson, I disagree. They are exactly as bad as they sound," Jean Pierre answered.

"Brats, they are," Mrs. Johnson said. "They wear my

nerves out. They disturb the hell out of me. But they'll grow out of those ways given time."

"Madame, living in this country, they most assuredly will not outgrow it. They cannot. They are sick, Madame. *C'est la maladie de l'hémisphère*—the sickness of this hemisphere."

"Jean Pierre." Madame Armand groaned. "Please, not now."

"Why not now?" Jean Pierre asked. Madame Armand threw up her hands in agitation.

"What sickness are you talking about?" Sarah asked.

"Slavery," Jean Pierre said. Mrs. Johnson laughed.

"Slavery? You can hardly accuse those middle-class, empty-headed brats of having any concern of slavery."

"Mais oui," Jean Pierre said. "I accuse them. That's all they think about. Their constant thought is to separate themselves from their slave past. *Voilà* the sickness."

He touched Sarah's cheek with the back of his hand. And his touch caused a confusing rush of blood throughout her body.

"Look at her, this child—so lovely, so talented. But she must suffer because she is not like the chameleon, ready to fade into the structure.

"Their scars are deep—so deep, they don't know they exist. It's part of them—their heartbeat. It shapes their lives, their—*comment dit-on?*—their thinking . . . the way they act, the way they see people. *Ce n'est pas vrai?*"

"You want to be with them, *n'est-ce pas?*" he asked Sarah. "You want to laugh with them, play with them, share their happiness, is that not so?"

He had moved his hand from her cheek. Sarah stilled the

97

urge to reach out, grab it, and put it back on her face, bury her lips in his palm. She wanted to say to him that yes, she had wanted their friendship but it didn't matter now.

"They are not so nice," Jean Pierre kept on. "Their heads are too filled with dreams of their rulers. They want to be like them. But you—you still exist. You make it difficult for them to have that dream."

"Come on," Mrs. Johnson laughed. "Sarah and Cathy have been friends for a long time—most of their lives."

"But your Cathy—she is not confused?"

"It's that boy Milton she's been seeing. His parents have him confused—but they have money."

"Clarice," Mama Dear said, "Cathy's always been a little that way. Reckon it's all our fault. But we got to face it.

"Her father being born and brought up here, don't you know. We didn't do right by him not letting him know the outside world. He couldn't adjust to it—out there. The pressure killed him—that's what did.

"See, Big Red and me, we was born fighting, what Jean Pierre call this disease. We were smack right in the middle of it.

"When we got here we reckoned we had reached heaven. We got into this house, and didn't want to leave. This house became 'the North' to us. Heaven. We had left the South—and hell.

"Li'l Jason's world started right here in this house. He didn't know but the Dixons' Quaker friends. He went to Quaker schools, played with Quaker children. We didn't even want him to know nothing about another world, another time. Sure, Big Red stayed mad and ranted and raved about the South. But them were just words to Li'l Jason.

"The pressure killed him. The pressure of being rejected, of not being a full man—after all the years of belonging, don't you know? Confused him—that confusion cause the pressure.

"Confusion is the way Cathy started out. I remember the time when Cathy ask me, 'Grandma, why you so black?' And I told her, 'I'm black like this so that you can be pretty as you is.' "

"Chère Mama"—Madame Armand spoke in astonishment—"your granddaughter, she love you, *non*?"

"My granddaughter, she loves me, yes." The old woman rocked the creaking rocker. "I'm the one grandmother she got. Clarice's folks took one good look at the man she married and disowned them—on the spot. Philadelphia big shots—don't you know. I recall when Cathy was so high"— Mama Dear measured inches from the floor—"her telling her li'l friends, 'That black lady's our housekeeper.' Clarice give her one good whack on her bottom. 'This lady is my mother-in-law, and Cathy's grandmother,' she told them kids."

"But, Mother, Cathy was so young—a baby," Mrs. Johnson protested. "She hadn't even begun to think good."

"Now she thinks good, madame?" Jean Pierre asked. "I don't think so. She's sick. She suffers the curse of the hemisphere!"

"Oh, come," Mrs. Johnson scoffed. "Don't tell me this curse, as you call it, doesn't exist in Africa."

"It has spread throughout the world. But it's here in these

Americas that it is a monster disease—a plague. It is here, *chère madame,* that there is no respect for history. No truth. The lessons of this hemisphere are new. It is the one hemisphere peopled entirely by expatriates from every country in the world. This drama in black and white is played out on soil beneath which the ravaged remains of its native peoples are interred. We refuse to see it. So we cannot talk about it —and so, *voilà*—confusion."

"Please, Jean Pierre." Mrs. Johnson gave a derisive little laugh. "Don't give historical significance to those children's shallow behavior."

"It is shallow at this age, but go one step further, madame, and it will be so profound . . ."

"Cathy's going through a phase in life that she's bound to outgrow."

"Mais oui." Madame nodded in sympathy. "And with Clarice, who understand."

"But do Clarice understand?" The old woman surprised them all by asking. Her face turned pensive. "Sometimes I do wonder . . ." She shook her head and kept rocking.

"Why do you say that?" Mrs. Johnson appeared upset by her mother-in-law's criticism.

"We know Cathy's the way she is," Mama Dear said as she kept rocking. "She's so much Big Red's blood that one can't hardly judge her. One got to understand Big Red when they know what went into making him. But Cathy ain't got no one to judge her because no one understand her. She ain't got no friends. All she got around her is worshipers. Clarice keep changing schools, changing houses. But that can only give to someone like Cathy, who's standing in the shallows—a profound confusion.

"To be sure, Big Red and me had come here ignorant and scared. But we known we was ignorant and I known I was scared. We didn't have to face up to it. We could go from there. But these kids got education to blind them. They don't know . . . don't know . . ." She kept shaking her head. "They got to get to a place and stop to take account of where, why, how . . .

"Look at Sarah. It ain't a problem to her. She sitting there playing—working—she'll make it."

Sarah blushed. She knew she was going to make it. Playing the piano had been ground into her for as long as she had thoughts to think. She had no choice. Being with Cathy had made it easier to stick to the rules of discipline—rules which had become Lottie's rules. Sarah loved Cathy. The friends that Cathy had collected along the way made it impossible to worship her. She did love her. Was that what Mama Dear meant?

"Court jester," Jean Pierre scoffed. "We entertain them and they take the bows. We are the gladiators and while we brag of our strength and greatness, we are moved like checkers on a board."

"My God, Jean Pierre, what a twisted mind," Mrs. Johnson cried. "Where in this world do people succeed without hard work?"

"Those who steal, madame. The colonialists."

"That was back then."

"That still is, madame."

"Look, we Black Americans have worked hard, Jean

Pierre. I have had to struggle for every inch of success I've ever achieved."

"Oui. For the wealth you can now achieve, the lands of our forefathers have been ravaged."

"Mon Dieu." Madame Armand threw up her hands in despair. *"Chère* Clarice, I beg you. Do not continue. You cannot win. No one can win when Jean Pierre talks about his Africa. He can go on forever."

Jean Pierre laughed and said to Sarah, *"C'est bizarre*—I can see so clearly what you in America have not yet begun to regard."

"America?" Madame Armand said. "It is not America." Her fan had gone back into use. "He is the same with his father. They fight. They make it impossible for father and son to live on one island. Fight, fight, fight. *Enfin,* even I must agree that it is best for Jean Pierre that he must leave —me, his home . . ."

Mama Dear's eyes were still bright with interest. She ignored Madame Armand to ask, "Jean Pierre, what do you see that we in this country cannot?"

"That knowing will erase some of the confusion, madame," Jean Pierre responded. "Our great tragedy is that we see Africa as a defeated wasteland. We blame ourselves for slavery. Our sin! But those who stole from us, from our ancestors, those who plunder our lands for gold, diamonds, zinc—we sing and dance for their pleasure and worship them for that wealth."

"Africa, Africa, Africa," Madame Armand wailed in exasperation. "I did not come to the States to sit in this house and talk Africa. It is enough that Africa has claimed my son. I will not have it eating my brains!"

Her angry outburst brought an instant silence that lasted to a stretch of seconds; then Mrs. Johnson said in a loud whisper, "Madame Armand, what will you like to do while you're here?"

"Sail," came the prompt reply. "We did all the time when I lived here. Madame Dixon and Big Red and the children. We all went to sail *n'est-ce pas,* Chère Mama?

"My Jean Pierre, he is a good sailor. On the island, before he leave, every day we sail. He had many friends—girls— and he takes them, so I go too. Now he's no more on the island." She shrugged. "But I want to go sailing, now that I have him." The two women drew closer on the couch, their voices lowered in the way of women who have struck the same chord.

Jean Pierre reached down to play with the keys of the piano, and Sarah moved to make room for him to sit. Together they picked out notes over the keyboard, blending them to create funny tunes that kept them laughing. Sarah admired his hands—big hands, long, lean fingers with square tips, the hands of a workingman. She also liked the strength of his arm, which kept rubbing against hers—hot, muscular. They went with his broad shoulders, against which she fought the impulse to lean. While they played and laughed, Mama Dear rocked, her bright curious eyes on them. Finally she leaned over to speak in a hushed voice, not wanting to disturb Madame Armand: "Jean Pierre, talk to me—tell me what we Americans can do about this curse which you talk about."

"We, Chère Mama, can lay claim to Africa—in our hearts. We can ask every child to give a penny, a nickel, a dime, a quarter, every week. And we can send it to Africa. That way, we help Africa develop, to become strong."

"Such a li'l bit of money? How can that help? We need governments—"

"No, no, Chère Mama. We must do this to raise the consciousness of the children here, to give to them respect for themselves and their homeland. It must be a cause, to help erase confusion."

"Is that your work?" Sarah asked.

"That's my dream," Jean Pierre said, and he smiled, looking into her eyes. "My work, along with philanthropic organizations and the United Nations, is to help rebuild the forests, try to reclaim the deserts."

"We used to send boxes to the needy in Africa," Mama Dear said, "—Master Dixon, Prudence, Big Red—and when you and your mother would come—"

"The Dixons were good people." Jean Pierre nodded. "It used to make me so happy to come here. I remember that once, like your son, I thought all Americans were like the Dixons."

"Have you seen their paintings in the brown-and-tan room?" Sarah asked. "They looked like good people. I wish I had had the chance to meet them."

"You would have liked them, and they, *mon amie,* would have adored you." His eyes flashed into hers. Sarah's body tingled. She tried to find words to answer him. How did one flirt?

A sudden clap of hands forced their eyes apart. Madame

Armand jumped to her feet. "Good," she cried. She rushed to throw her arms around her son. *"Oui, mon chou,* we have settled everything for you."

"Quoi?" Jean looked around. "Mama, what did you do? What did you settle for me?" he cried, alarmed.

"Tomorrow, *mon chéri.* We shall go sailing. You and me. Clarice and Sarah and Chère Mama. How wonderful—no more quarrels. No more talk about Africa. We'll steal tomorrow and hide away—then we can be happy, *n'est-ce pas?"*

"Impossible!" Jean Pierre frowned at his mother. "Mama, we did discuss this. You know that I am here to work. Tomorrow I am expecting a call . . ."

"But that is why we must steal, *n'est-ce pas?* Telephones make you crazy. They will only take you away from Mama —and Sarah," she said with a wicked smile. "Jean Pierre, after the terrible experience she had today, we want to make Sarah smile, *n'est-ce pas?"*

"Mama." Jean Pierre intended to scold, but her childlike quality exasperated him. He turned to Sarah. "You see . . ." Sarah, too, looked at him with round, brown, sorrowful eyes. Silenced, he asked with a gesture of futility, "But where shall I find a boat?"

"Not to worry," Mama Dear said, rocking hard to make the chair creak. "Alicia's father has a boat tied up at the yacht club. I'll fix things. When do you want it? Tomorrow morning early, *n'est-ce pas?"*

Nine

 The feelings of being wanted and wanting to be wanted cannot be compared. Sarah awoke with a thrill of anticipation. She jumped out of bed and rushed to the drawer to take out the white-on-white bikini she had been longing to wear. She slipped it on, then stood admiring her long, slender body, her slim midriff, her rounded behind, liking the contrast of her dark skin against the white. After slipping into white slacks, she went downstairs glowing with confidence. She entered the kitchen, where Madame Armand sat drinking coffee, and stood waiting for her to look up.

"Mais," Madame Armand said, *"tu est belle ce matin . . .* very pretty." Sarah flushed with pleasure, loving the woman.

Madame Armand also startled the eyes, in a red bathing

suit beneath a bright red printed African wrap, which heightened the redness of her skin.

"You want coffee?" asked Madame Armand, pouring out a cup for Sarah. Just then Jean Pierre came in—dazzling in white T-shirt, shorts, and sneakers. A sense of unreality took hold of Sarah—more unreal than her own fantasy world. How had this day come about—that she, Sarah Richardson, had been chosen by whatever gods to spend the day with this tall, dark, so very handsome man?

"Where—are the others?" she heard herself ask, even though she hoped that they had not been included.

"They're asleep. Had a big night last night," Mrs. Johnson answered, coming into the room. "I thought of asking them to come along—but not one of them stirred."

"Now, don't y'all look like a bouquet of flowers," Mama Dear said from the kitchen door. "So fresh, and so ready to have yourselves a ball."

"What are you doing?" Mrs. Johnson asked. "Aren't you coming?"

Mother Dear had dressed for the garden, in her long dress and wide-brimmed hat. In her hands she carried a shears.

"No, it's been a while since I even thought of leaving this house. Never want to anymore. I loves my home, loves to putter making things remain the way I wants them to."

"Chère Mama, but I'll take good care. I'm a very good sailor."

"We want you with us," Madame Armand said. "You can just sit—we'll do all."

"My mother-in-law hates risks," Mrs. Johnson said. "She takes it slow because she wants to live forever."

"Long's I can." Mama Dear laughed. "Who's going to take up time with my ghosts—and my flowers—if something happens? Anyway, I got to get busy getting breakfast for Cathy and the rest of 'em. Got to cheer 'em up. Can't you see 'em—mouths all poked out when they know you gone boating?"

"I called Cathy," Mrs. Johnson said, and Sarah's stomach dropped with disappointment. "But she didn't even budge."

"Alicia'll meet y'all at the club. Her father's working, but she knows how to handle things. Depend on her."

And so they drove off, waving to Mama Dear, standing on the porch in the cool morning air with her shears in hand, waving. They arrived at the club and found Alicia already waiting.

"We hate to do this to you," Mrs. Johnson said. "Not only do we keep you up nights, now we intrude into your early-morning sleep."

"S'okay," Alicia said, shrugging. "I'll go back to bed—read or something. Say," she said to Sarah, "what about that book?"

"I didn't finish," Sarah said. "But it doesn't matter. I'll let you have it later."

Alicia led them down to the pier and they anchored the boat. "It's twenty-four feet, with lots of space—a lark to maneuver," she explained. "We haven't been out much this summer—except on weekends."

The worry shadowing Jean Pierre's face disappeared, as he examined the compact chrome-plated fiber glass craft. His spirits visibly rose. How wonderful to see.

Using the motor, he maneuvered the craft around other

sailboats and cabin cruisers anchored in the marina. They cruised into open waters. As Jean Pierre readied the sails, Sarah put on sunglasses to observe him without being obvious. Then they were off. She closed her eyes as the boat picked up speed, and put back her head to enjoy the rush of wind and the spray of salt water sprinkling her face. She thought of the tankers, the freighters, sailing up and down the Hudson River on which she had dreamed of sailing. This had to be the most exciting experience of her life— sailing on this boat, with this man. What dream had ever been its equal?

"*Ca-pi-taine, Ca-pi-taine . . .*" Madame Armand's voice roused Sarah. She opened her eyes to see Madame Armand stretched out on deck in her undersized bikini, over which her buxom flesh pushed, waving up to the yacht next to them. "*Ca-pi-taine,* but you are too beautiful," she called, her small teeth exposed in wide-mouthed laughter. "Your hair, *c'est* absolutely *magnifique* . . ."

Indeed, the captain, with epaulettes on his white jacket, was a tall, heavyset man with a face burnished red by the sun and wind and lined by age, and possessed a wonderful head of thick white hair.

"I thank you kindly, ma'am," he called down to her. "For that compliment let me offer you some champagne." He held up a bottle, just as the sail caught a wind and they glided away. Madame Armand called back, "Hold it for me —we'll be back, *mon ca-pi-taine. . . .*"

Sarah laughed, loud, free laughter. Who better to be out in the world with than this woman in her too-small swimsuit, in which she looked so sexy, talking to strangers and making it appear that that was the way of things?

Madame Armand's face glowed, her untied hair blowing in the wind. Sarah felt a fleeting sadness. How much she had missed in this life: the old house, Mama Dear, this woman—her son. She had never known in this world that a Madame Armand, that a Jean Pierre, existed.

Sarah turned to Jean Pierre, studying him at the sails— somber, sunk deep in his thoughts. He seemed more like the parent than the son. To him laughter didn't come easy.

Mrs. Johnson, in her two-piece blue suit, with the slim body of a model, was eclipsed by the voluptuous woman.

Frivolous? No. Sarah liked Mrs. Johnson—always had. Yet now that she had met Madame Armand, Mrs. Johnson had seemed drained of substance, just as Fred Hamilton had appeared to be without substance the moment Jean Pierre had come on the scene.

The women stripped off the tops of their swimsuits and lay with their bare backs to the sun. That gave Sarah the courage to slip off her slacks, putting her white-on-white bikini on display. She sat on the bench with her back against the side of the boat, watching Jean Pierre adjusting the sails—his dark arms, their muscles moving just beneath the skin, gave him grace and authority. She sighed, then looked away as a pride of swans glided up to the boat. The long-necked, graceful creatures gazed back at her with curiosity, until a stiff breeze pushed the boat along.

Other sailboats in the distance resembled paintings against the horizon. An occasional speedboat racing a distance away left a wake that cradled them, then left them once again. Listing on the smooth surface of water, they waited for another push from the wind.

Sarah finally found something to say. "Jean Pierre, tell me more about Africa."

"It's beautiful," he said, smiling.

"From documentaries we see that the animals of Africa are always interesting. But the portrayals of the people are so—so negative."

"In what way?"

"They are usually underpaid servants, following wealthy whites with heavy bundles on their heads—on safaris."

"That happens too," he said. "But is that what you want to talk about, the people of Africa?"

His eyes smiled. They roved over her body, down to her feet, then up to her mouth. He stared at her mouth, then rested on her eyes. Sarah blushed. Her face burned and a quick sweat pushed through her pores. Seeing sweat running down the sides of her face in the cool breeze, Jean Pierre threw back his head and laughed.

The women never stirred. They were asleep. "Well, where do I start? You know, of course, that Africa is the oldest civilization in the world. Life started there. In Africa we have all the contrasts in the world—the most interesting people. We have the tallest men in the world, we also have the shortest. We have the largest, most docile beasts in the world, and also the smallest, most ravenous insects. All the fish in the world spawn in African ports."

"Yet Africa is so poor," Sarah protested.

"No. You are wrong. Africa is so rich. It's the richest continent in the world. In its soil, gold, diamonds, uranium, iron, rubber, platinum, aluminum—everything is to be found there. Africa is very rich. It's the people who are poor."

"Rich in the same sense as Europe? The United States?"

"Europe, the United States, could not be so rich, if not for Africa's wealth."

"And—so the people are poor . . ."

"Ahhh, so you understand, my little Sarah." Grabbing her hand, he pulled her to her feet and they stood, thighs touching. "Sarah, you are talented, brilliant—of course, you must have these feelings too."

What feelings? Was his body burning too? Was his heart beating as hard as hers? Or was he still talking about Africa? More questions of Africa spun around in her mind. She wanted to hear about its history, its music. But more, she wanted him to make her understand the things that were happening to her—in her.

"I care," Jean Pierre said. "Deeply, I care." The pressure of his arms around her, pulling her closer, left her perplexed. Cared about what? Africa? Or her, standing so close that she had to hold her breath? But they had only just met.

"What do we do about it?" she whispered.

He looked out over the water, shrugged. "I am no politician," he said. "I know only that I must work!"

"Oh—your work," Sarah said, suddenly desolate.

"Yes, I have to reclaim the land from the desert. Work to secure our forests. Africa must feed herself! Clothe herself! Politics? I shall leave that for my children."

"Children!" How did it happen that here she was thinking about sex, while his mind wrapped around earth-shaking things? She moved away from him. A breeze blew through the emptiness between them. Sarah sat, and as the breeze whipped at the sails, they talked.

"In Africa we have much to do," he said, "—build more schools, train our children. Politics will have to wait until I get children."

"Oh—so you have no children?"

"Me? No. Children must wait until I have a wife."

Once again he searched through her eyes. Sarah looked away. His shift in moods unbalanced her. They never appeared to be talking about the same things. Had he just talked about marriage? To her? But she hardly knew him. Obviously, they didn't understand each other.

"Do you detest us—Black Americans?" she asked. "Because we go to school and still seem so . . . shallow? Is that why you call us court jesters?"

"Detest?"

"Yes, you seem to imply that we're selling out Africa."

"Mais non." Jean Pierre shook his head and once again aimed his black eyes into hers. "It is Africa who sold you out. Do you know how many of our people were sold into slavery by jealous kings? Our great thinkers, musicians, our warriors . . . We cannot help being a great people," he said. "All you have to guard against here is that they do not kill the spirit. You have brought the soul here, to stay for eternity. The spirit—it must survive."

He laughed, an angry, bitter laugh. "My father, he is a fool. He can do so much for his people—but he works only for money. And your friends—they are fools, imbeciles. They cannot see that you are the best in them. And so they are jealous—because you are beautiful, and have talent, and are African.

"It's the curse of this hemisphere!" he cried, and Madame Armand sat up.

"What—what is it?" Heavy breasts heaved. She looked out over the water. "Jean Pierre, you have already turned back?"

Sarah tore her eyes away from the woman's lovely bosom and looked over the water to see the boats moored in the distance. Indeed, they had turned back and she hadn't noticed.

"I close my eyes," Madame Armand said. "And there you are talking about the curse again, and thinking about your phone calls, *n'est-ce pas*? What to do with this son of mine?"

"It is the hour," Jean Pierre said. "I bring you back to have time for your swim."

They had already been out for hours. Amazing how quickly the day had gone by, without seeming to have passed at all. But suddenly she knew the time had gone; she was hungry.

"Hold the sails so that I can go in. I must swim to shore," Madame Armand said, adjusting the top of her suit, and stood ready to dive in.

"The water is cold here—not like your island waters," Mrs. Johnson warned as she herself stood up, also ready to dive in. "At any rate the tide is going in. That will help us."

Madame Armand dived into the water and looked back at them, shouting, *"Ayeee, mais comme c'est froid, mon Dieu."*

Mrs. Johnson hit the water and looked back laughing.

114

"Damn right it's cold," she said. "Jean Pierre, don't you stay too far behind. It's been some time since I swam so far."

"Why do you not go with them, Sarah?" Jean Pierre asked.

"I can't swim," Sarah answered.

"Quoi? Mais ce n'est pas possible," Jean Pierre said. "That's the first lesson a child must learn."

"On your island, maybe. But not on the island where I was born," Sarah said. "But I want to learn. More than anything—but I don't get the chance."

"But you have the chance—here. I'll give you the chance. I will show you."

Sarah looked out at the heads of the two women, swimming, talking, becoming specks in the distance. They made swimming look so relaxed, so easy. "Will you?" she asked.

"I insist," Jean Pierre answered. "You are so very special to me, Sarah. You play the piano. You speak languages. You flirt so well with those pretty brown eyes. I insist you must swim."

Sweat broke out on her thighs, making her realize that they were again touching his. She moved her leg away from his quickly. He laughed.

Ten

"Swimming lessons?" Mrs. Johnson said as they drove back to the house. "Great chance for you, Sarah. And from the look on your face I can tell you'll hang around for a bit. Why don't you wait until after I'm gone and let's have a few more days of sailing? I haven't had this much fun for a long time. I'm so glad you came when you did, Madame Armand."

"C'est fantastique, n'est-ce pas?" Madame Armand said. "Nothing in the world is better than sailing."

"Sarah, do you mind putting off your lessons for a day or two?"

"Not at all, Mrs. Johnson," Sarah said. She didn't. She, too, had never enjoyed anything so much as the sail with Jean Pierre beside her, their thighs touching. Her body tingled still. She felt happy, yet confused; unsettled, yet excited. The world kept opening and she wanted to enjoy every part of it. When Jean Pierre looked into her eyes, no words came to her to express the lightness of spirit she felt.

All during dinner, relaxed from the day spent in the sun and wind, they laughed and joked and ate Mama Dear's fish soup by the bowlful.

"I'm glad you enjoy my friends," Mama Dear said to Sarah. "I knew you would. Even when Madame Armand was ready to kill herself, that long time ago, she always made us laugh."

"She's wonderful," Sarah said. "She flirts. She had the captain of a big yacht pouring champagne for us."

"Only in the morning," Madame Armand reminded her. "In the evening I look for him but—like the wind, puff, he is not there." Her pouting lips managed to make their funny adventure seem tragic. "That is the way of men, *chérie.* Still, I want my champagne, *n'est-ce pas?*"

"I'll go into town and get some," Jody offered.

"And you, when you come back, will you have a beautiful thick head of white hair? That must be the man who pours my champagne."

They shouted with laughter, and the mood throughout the evening remained gay. Sarah laughed more than she had ever laughed. Cathy too. But Sarah sensed the underlying resentment in Cathy's laughter. It didn't matter. She refused to let anything upset her. Nor did she look directly at Cathy all evening. Instead, she looked past her to the head of the table, where Jean Pierre sat, looking at her, flirting. She, too, flirted and blushed. Later, when Cathy and her friends had gone out, Sarah floated upstairs. She had no doubt that she had fallen in love with the handsomest, most perfect man in the entire world.

For the next few days it was the same. Sarah awoke before Cathy and friends, and along with Mrs. Johnson and the Armands went sailing in weather "commanded by the gods," Madame Armand said. Sunlight days sprinkled with clouds softened the harsh rays; wonderful breezes pushed them along the smooth surface of water. When the winds died, their boat idled, or rocked in the wake of occasional speed- or tugboats.

On the third day, stretched out beside Jean Pierre, watching the bobbing heads of the two women growing smaller as they neared the shore, Sarah said, "Mrs. Johnson will be leaving in a few days."

"*Oui*—then we shall see about your swimming lessons."

"I don't care anymore about swimming," Sarah said. "I have fallen in love with sailing."

"Me too. I am content," Jean Pierre agreed. "Today I am somebody else. But tomorrow, the day after, the telephone, it will ring—and then business, business. Today I don't want to know about it. Yesterday and today, I am the spoiled child. These days are special to me."

"To me too," Sarah agreed. "I don't want your phone calls tomorrow. I don't want Mrs. Johnson to leave. I want every day to be like it has been."

"*Mais, chérie*—we must learn you to swim. That's important, *n'est-ce pas?*" Sarah remained silent, smiling. Yes, important, but nothing was more important than being stretched out beside him, feeling him there.

"Sarah, you are too sweet. So gentle. There are no women

like you in the world—talented yet timid. Innocent yet sensual. And so—so . . ." He gazed through her eyes. "You are too beautiful a woman, Sarah Richardson."

A woman? His woman? The unsettling look in his eyes demanded that she be his woman. Her own desire, pulling and tugging at her insides, demanded that she be a woman —a beautiful woman. But even lying next to him, touching him, she lacked the ease, the familiarity, needed to accept herself as a complete woman.

Silently, Sarah gazed up at the sky and into the sprawling bits and pieces of clouds. The boat rocked. Water slapped against its sides, inducing a kind of trance. In the tranquility she combed through her mind. How could she make herself the complete woman that he thought her, that she desired to be? How much time would it take? Days and days of sailing and thinking? Sarah sighed.

That night Jean Pierre's long-awaited call came. The next day he waited at home for follow-up calls. Taking advantage of the time, Mrs. Johnson went shopping for souvenirs and Madame Armand made up for her days of negligence by helping Mama Dear in the gardens.

Sarah had not forgotten her promise to give Alicia *The Bluest Eye*. She decided to spend her time finishing it. She spent the day in the brown-and-tan room reading, only to find that she had lost her power of concentration. After having turned fifty fruitless pages, and seeing only Jean Pierre's face, she gave up, and was about to go downstairs when Cathy came into the room.

"Just what do you think you're doing, Sarah Richardson?" Standing her back to the door, her face twisted in anger, smoky eyes lit, nostrils flaring, hands opening and closing into fists, she looked like the incarnation of evil.

"What do you mean?" Sarah stood with her back to the desk, facing her.

"You know damn well what I mean! I'm talking about Jean Pierre! Just what are you trying to pull?"

"I'm not trying to pull anything, Cathy," Sarah said, without intending to she had put the emphasis on *trying.*

"Oh—you think that you have done it? That carrying on with him out on the boat means that you have it made with him?"

"I don't know what you mean," Sarah said. "Everybody knows that we have been going sailing—your mother, Madame—"

"Don't give me that. Just how do you manage to get them to leave you alone with Jean Pierre?"

"That's their own doing," Sarah said.

"It's planned. I know a plan when I see one." Cathy walked up to Sarah and stood with her face pushed up to hers. Sarah stepped back, trying to keep calm.

"Look, Cathy, your mother and Madame Armand like to swim to shore, and someone has to bring back the boat."

"So—now you're a sailor!"

"Please, Cathy, don't—"

"Miss goody, goody bullshit artist. I didn't want you here, but you worked your magic on Mother. Now that you are here, you think you can steal the show."

"I think no such thing."

"Well, you can't!" Cathy cried. "How can you even start

to think that Jean Pierre can be interested in you while I'm around?"

Sarah hadn't believed it. She still found it hard to believe. Still she knew he liked her. Loved her?

"I can see through you," Cathy said. "You knew I had my eyes on him. Don't tell me you didn't. I never kept that a secret."

"Neither did you keep it a secret that you liked Milt—and Fred," Sarah said.

"What are you trying to insinuate?" Cathy's eyes narrowed. She put her fists up, forcing Sarah to step away again. She didn't want to fight. Yet she didn't want to back down. She had no reason to back down.

"What are you and your friends trying to insinuate about me?" she asked.

"We don't have to insinuate. We know all about you. You're jealous."

"Me? Jealous?"

"Yes, of me—because I refuse to turn my back on them."

"But it's okay for you to turn your back on me, Cathy? Why do you call me a friend? Because you can come around when you need me."

"Need you!"

"Yes, to help you with your lessons."

"Girl, you got to be kidding. I got lots of friends who can help me out with lessons. It's Mother who makes me go to you for help."

"Your mother? Why? If you don't want to?"

"Because she swears out that you're some kind of whiz kid. And because she wants to make believe that the breakup with your mother isn't for real. But I don't need you, Sarah Richardson. I don't appreciate you always running after me."

"Do I run after you, Cathy?"

"What do you call it when you come uninvited to tea at my house? That's running. When you come to my grandmother's house knowing I don't want you—that's running."

"I—I didn't know you were having tea," Sarah said. "Not on that day."

"At least your mother knew when to stay away from where she wasn't wanted," Cathy said.

"My mother? What are you talking about?"

"I'm talking about when my mother told her she didn't want her around. She had enough sense to stay away. But no matter what I say or do, you're still around like some goddamn dog at my heels. Why don't you go back home and leave us alone!"

Cathy's hatred seared through Sarah. It singed her heart. She had loved this girl—as much as she loved her family. More, perhaps. Her family was given. Cathy, like her music, was the chosen. Sarah searched through the smoldering blue eyes that now were almost black from anger for a semblance of the love they had once shared. She saw only hatred. "We were so close, Cathy—sisters. What happened to change that?"

"People change," Cathy snapped. "They grow up. Not you. You stay the same. Child genius. The great talent. God, how I detest seeing you blush and grin every time someone says, 'Look at that sweet, talented Sarah. How hard she works.' Overdoing, overdoing. My God, don't you ever get tired?"

"Cathy, you're jealous of me?" Cathy had had all the opportunities to play, to excel.

"Who? Me? Jealous? I get attention without scene stealing. My friends and I are sophisticated. Or hadn't you noticed? We're grown. We go wherever we want, do whatever we want to do. We don't need you hanging around raising questions."

"Questions? What questions?"

"Are they? Or aren't they? Should we? Or shouldn't we? Nobody knows. Nobody cares. We're admitted wherever we go—without having to beg or being insulted. We're accepted, Sarah Richardson—so long as you're not tagging along."

Sarah felt herself growing smaller, smaller. The pain in her chest grew bigger, bigger. Milt. Sheila. She knew they placed a high premium on color. Not Cathy. Never Cathy. Wicked? Yes. Devilish? Yes. Mean? Yes. But never color conscious. Sarah shook her head in disbelief.

She and Cathy had lain side by side, on the same bed, listened in on their parents' meetings when Peace and Brotherhood and Black Is Beautiful were slogans with meaning. How had Cathy changed that much?

Cathy watched the pain dig deep in Sarah, then walked out of the room. Sarah, her temples throbbing, staggered out to the terrace. She stood staring out into the woods. And Lottie—what had Cathy said about Lottie?

Sarah gazed into the tangle of branches. Birds chirped, dry leaves rustled. She tried to follow the twistings and turnings of those determined branches, to keep her mind blank. Then the long branch reaching over to the terrace gave the rail a slap. Startled, Sarah stared down at the branch. She had indeed lost a friend, one that she had loved and had tried to hold on to. So why the feeling of emptiness. But what had Cathy said about her mother?

Leaving the room, Sarah went downstairs and out to the porch. Milt and Jody were out there sitting on the steps, playing cards with Sheila and Betty. When Sarah came out, Betty looked up from her hand. "I thought you'd still be out sailing," she said.

Betty had become more attractive now that her skin had burned to bronze and her hair was streaked copper.

"We didn't go sailing today," Sarah answered.

"We stayed at home too," Betty said. "We had a bit too much sun yesterday. By the way, we saw Mrs. Johnson and Madame Armand swimming in from the boat. A fun thing to do."

"Yes." Sheila looked up. "I understand they left you with Jean Pierre—sailing."

"Play your cards, Sheila," Milt growled.

"Why didn't you swim back with them?" Betty asked. "Or was something happening on board that we ought to know?"

"I can't swim," Sarah answered.

"Do tell," Sheila drawled. "How does anyone live so long and not know how to swim?"

Silently, Sarah looked at Sheila. Of all Cathy's friends she had liked Sheila the least. Now she didn't care. None of

Cathy's friends mattered now that her friendship with Cathy had ended so definitively.

"Come off it, Sheila," Milt sneered. "Inner-city folks don't go near water, how do you expect them to swim?" He looked at Sheila, his eyes sliding around in their sockets as though they were greased.

"Well, I hope you took the opportunity to at least get a good squeeze." Betty laughed. "That Jean Pierre's got to be the handsomest dude ever."

"Squeeze?" Sheila scoffed. "You must be joking, Betty. Those senior citizens swimming off gave our Frenchman the chance he needed. The French invented lovemaking, don't you know. Want to tell us about it, Sarah?"

"And what makes you think that Jean Pierre would want to make love to Sarah?" Cathy and Fred had come to the doorway. Cathy glared at Sheila, her anger obvious. "Just because he feels sorry for her doesn't mean he wants her!"

Her utter disregard for Fred standing next to her or for Milt lying at her feet, surprised them all. The card players hid their embarrassment in their cards. But Fred decided to goad Cathy: "Anyhow, Sarah," he said, "I sure hope you're having yourself one hell of a ball."

"I am," Sarah answered. "I'm having a delightful time."

"Having a delightful time," Sheila mimicked. "I wonder what dear Grandmother will think of her precious, talented virgin, Saint Sarah, flaunting herself over the waves like a flag. Delighted, I'll bet."

"Watch that, Sheila," Fred growled, stopping their laughter. "Don't start no shit and there'll be none. Them that smears is usually the ones smelling shitty."

He stalked back into the house, leaving them mired in silence. Cathy's jealous outburst had found a mark.

Later at dinner, their laughter amazed Sarah. How quickly they forgot. Eating, talking, laughing. They had pushed away slurs, jealousies, and confrontations, or so it seemed. Was that sophistication? Was that growing up? Then Sarah thought, *I still haven't grown up.* For her the events of the afternoon still left a bad taste. And from the expression on Cathy's face she hadn't forgotten either.

Inwardly, Sarah quivered. What if Jean Pierre had heard their remarks, and learned the depth of their resentment against her? He might change his mind—his feelings toward her. She glanced to the head of the table in agony. Once she caught Jean Pierre looking back. The black centers of his eyes twinkled. She looked away in relief. Still, she wished he were beside her.

"Did you ever see anything so funny?" Sheila said, laughing. "Remember when Milt stood on his hands in the sand, those long, bony legs unsteady in the air, his toes clawing."

"Like a crab," Betty said, giggling.

"Exactly . . ."

"I am a crab," Milt cried louder than was warranted.

"A great big crab with big claws—the better to grab you." Playfully, he stretched clawed fingers over the table at Cathy. She squealed in childish delight. There followed an exchange of teasing and light banter. "Careful, careful, Milt, or this Galahad'll declaw you," Cathy said as she pointed toward Fred with her chin. "Hadn't you noticed how he just loves going to the rescue of lewd ladies in distress?"

"And who, may I ask, is the lewd lady who is so distressed?" Jean Pierre demanded. His question brought a sudden silence. Eyes turned to Sarah, glinting with humor or animosity. In panic Sarah stared down at her empty plate. Someone attempted to laugh. Betty? Jody? Cathy succeeded, with loud hysterical laughter.

Sarah searched into Jean Pierre's eyes.

Mama Dear jumped to her feet. "We are at the end of a too relaxing day," she said. "A day when idleness made for a bit of evilness—*n'est-ce pas*?

"Anyway, the week didn't go too badly, did it? You young ones played in the sand—crabbing, grabbing, and clawing. Madame Armand and my dearest daughter-in-law found they had much in common and dear, dear Sarah and Jean Pierre got to setting one another's eyes just aglittering. Sure did. So let's top off this day listening to Sarah play us some of her pretty songs. You don't mind, do you, Sarah honey?"

Indeed, she did mind. The attack had left the taste of ash in her mouth. Sarah looked at the old woman, who stood inviting them to leave the table. She held her back straight, so unrelenting. In her long print cotton dress, with her head of white hair held so high, no one could tell that she had suffered enough to make Sarah's suffering—adolescent. So Sarah left the table and led the rest of them into the parlor.

She sat at the piano, moved her fingers over the keyboard, and the strange feeling came over her. Mama Dear had lived so long that she had become a fairy godmother or a witch. How else could she read so clearly the thoughts and sentiments that went flittering around the old house?

They sang together songs intended to transcend barriers:

"Che Sarà, Sarà"; "Alouette"; "Funiculí Funiculá" . . .
Jean Pierre, standing beside the piano, gave her his
strength. He kept looking at her, his eyes constantly saying:
Are you all right? Is everything okay? And Sarah kept answer-
ing with a nod, a smile. All indeed appeared to be ending
well. Then Madame Armand said, "Jean Pierre, *chéri.* I
make Clarice the promise. I tell her to give us one more day
and you will take us sailing."

"Mama, you know I might have to leave for the city tomorrow."

"Jean Pierre, please. Just one more day? Do your mama
ask too much? Give me this one last day with my Clarice.
We might never see her again."

"I can't put off my work."

"Just this one time—for me?"

"Perhaps," Jean Pierre said in exasperation.

"And me?" Cathy asked. She had been sitting beside
Milt. Now she came and stood directly in front of Jean
Pierre.

"Pardon?" Jean Pierre said, taking a step back.

"I don't see why you think you have to take only Sarah. I
want to go sailing too."

Wild, exciting, smoldering with passion and jealousy,
Cathy gazed up at Jean Pierre. He stepped back again, perplexed, then looked at her friends.

"Yes," she said. "I want you to take me sailing." Jean
Pierre smiled.

"But, of course, with pleasure. But Milt . . ." He looked
directly over at the lanky unhappy young man. "The boat, it
is so small. Perhaps if you can secure a bigger one, for six.

Are you not six? Then we shall all go. Will you inquire from Alicia?"

"A wonderful idea," Mrs. Johnson said, jumping to her feet to lessen Jean Pierre's embarrassment. "If you guys can manage to get up early, what say we have a race?"

Cathy whirled around to confront her mother. Mrs. Johnson avoided her daughter's eyes. "Actually," she went on, "we haven't done anything together in all the time I've been here. A sailing competition ought to be real hip—the grand send-off."

"Voilà." Jean Pierre opened up his arms in an expansive show of relief. "All is settled. Milt, you make arrangements for the boat, and Cathy, she shall have her chance to sail."

"But, Mrs. Johnson," Milt wailed. "I don't know how to sail. I have never been sailing in my life."

"Well, as sophisticated as you are, I'd think one of you ought to know." Silence greeted that remark, so she said to Fred, "What about you, Fred?"

"I have no intention of going sailing—not tomorrow, or ever," Fred snapped. "In all probability, Mrs. Johnson, I'll spend the day on the beach, and if you don't mind, I'll drive back to the city with you."

The others sat quietly looking down at their hands. Cathy and her friends were no longer bold, aggressive, or given to indiscretions. They appeared fragile, vulnerable. Sarah turned back to the piano. "What song would you like to hear?" she asked.

"Please, enough is enough," Sheila cried, jumping to her feet. Then to her friends, "What do you guys say? Tina Turner. She's at the club tonight."

Eleven

A full moon. Its light spilled softly down, giving dimension to Mama Dear's garden. It
added shadows to the paths, to the cars
parked in the driveway. Sarah and Jean Pierre
stood watching from the porch as Cathy and friends piled
into their cars, slammed the doors, then raced away. They
waited until they heard the sounds fading—fading in the
distance. Then their fingers interlaced and they walked
down the steps, rounding the house onto the path alongside
the woods.

Moonlight guided them as they searched for the most
accessible entry into the forest. They walked beneath the
terrace of the brown-and-tan room. Sarah looked up and
thought of her quarrel with Cathy. She remembered staring
into the tangle of branches—branches as twisted as the tan-

gled web of circumstances that had made Cathy her friend
—a web she hadn't yet thought through.

Clearly she, Sarah, had needed the friendship more.
Their bonding had made bearable the anguish of loneliness
in her life of self-imposed discipline. But hadn't there been
times when Cathy needed her? Or had she been only a
challenge to Cathy—the one person who didn't bend to
Cathy's will, and whom she therefore intended to break?

"Pourquoi est-ce que tu es triste?" Jean Pierre asked. Sad?
Did she look sad?

"It's Cathy. I think she likes you," she said.

"Ce n'est pas vrai—not true," Jean Pierre said. "Your
Cathy doesn't like me. She detests you. There is a difference."

"How did you know?"

"Mais, c'est naturel. You are too beautiful."

"Cathy's the beautiful one," Sarah protested.

"But you are more so. Cathy sees you are more beautiful."

"No, she doesn't. Cathy thinks of me as . . ." A new
light suddenly cast a brightness over her relationship with
Cathy—past and present. . . .

"She want to see you as ugly. *C'est l'habitude.* Cathy *wants*
to think that you have no right to beauty. But she has good
eyes. She can see. Is she not an egoist?"

They plunged into the darkness. Jean Pierre, his arms
around her, guided her among the trees. They heard the
quickening of movement created by their presence—the
frightened squawk of abruptly awakened birds, the rustling
of animals in the underbrush.

"You seem to know the way," Sarah whispered. The darkness, the movement of unknown creatures, created a conspiratorial atmosphere.

"Ah, oui." He sighed, contented. "These woods I did play in as a child—with Chère Mama. Big Red had cleared it for her and she knows every tree, every limb. It used to be hers —then ours. The boys had grown—and she still enjoyed here, and so she was so kind to share with me. It is too beautiful—wait, you'll see."

"Seeing it with you will be like exploring a forest in Africa," she said, and he laughed long and loud. Excited animals chattered, the night sounds picked up momentum, then was a hush as though a giant hand had descended to strike them all still.

They pushed on through the thick-growing trees, leaning one on the other as their bodies brushed against each other in the dark. Then suddenly they stepped out of the dense woods into a circle of light. Moonlight.

"You see how it is beautiful," Jean Pierre said, holding her hand, guiding her over the soft, sandy earth. Sarah leaned against him, lonely for him, wanting him to be the person to whom she belonged. Like she had wanted to be with Cathy?

Her friendship with Cathy had been habit more than a joy. She had nothing to take its place. With Cathy she had had the right to fight, to demand—whether the demand had been respected or not. But with Jean Pierre?

"When will you be going away?" she asked.

"To Africa? Soon. I have meetings, contracts. In a few

days, a few weeks—soon. Then I shall take Mama home, visit my papa, fight with him—then I shall leave for Africa."

He stopped walking, turned her to face him. "You have heard of Henri Christophe, *non?*" he asked.

"Of Haiti?" Jean Pierre nodded.

"You know what he was always saying?"

"So much to do and so little time to do it?" Sarah asked.

"Precisely. He was correct. He spoke for me too. We—none of us—if we live for one hundred years—have time to do what must be done."

Sarah gazed up at him. How beautiful he looked by moonlight. Its softness had erased the harsh edges from his face, which she remembered now only because they were absent: his frown, which made his face so strong, the lines at the sides of his nose that promised to deepen with the years. His face held only softness, the beauty he must have had when Mama Dear first knew him.

"You are talking about your work?"

"Always. Always I talk about my work—and Africa. What else can I do in this one lifetime?"

On an impulse Sarah cupped his face with her hands. He bent down. Their lips touched and she moved away. Her blood pounded against her ears, her body shook. Then she heard a strange sound. "Is that water I hear?" she asked.

"Yes. The pond—its source . . ."

They walked on, their thighs brushing. And the desire that spread through her made her weak. Her heart pounded, pounded, and she had to remind herself to breathe. The ache at the pit of her stomach created a sensation too difficult to define.

"The pond, it is silent. But it has a source." He pointed beyond the trees facing them. "It's on the other side of that forest. It makes the brouhaha. It spouts between rocks—but where it begins nobody knows. It's magic." He grinned, and his grin reminded her of Mama Dear.

"Come, I want to see the pond and throw pebbles into it. Mama Dear says if it ripples a certain way after we throw pebbles, our wish will come true."

"So it is said," Jean Pierre agreed.

"Have you made wishes in the pond?"

"Hundreds of them."

"And have they come true?"

"Most," he said, and grinned, which made her wonder if he was telling the truth or teasing.

"Let's make a wish now," she said.

"Okay," Jean Pierre responded. Then he reached up and grabbed her arms, pulling her back. "That is the pond." He pointed to a wide area of darkness at their feet.

"But it's so dark," Sarah said. "It doesn't reflect the moonlight."

"It is magic," Jean Pierre said, still holding her. He kissed her then. "Now, that is my very first wish in this pond and it is the last one to come true. But then I was a little boy. *Et voilà*—the woman I love."

"True?" she asked. But it no longer mattered. He kissed her again. Her arms went around his neck. She held him, held his lips on hers, kissed him back—hard. Nothing and no one else mattered. Being in the moonlight with this man, Jean Pierre, feeling his hands, strong, deliberate, pulling her into him, holding her buttocks, pushing into her. Overwhelmed, she cried, "Stop. Stop." She pulled away, when she wanted to stay. He held her, knowing she wanted to stay. "Don't, Jean Pierre—please. . . ."

Like a doll she rested in his arms. "If you keep on I won't be able to stop."

"And you want to stop, *chérie?*"

"I must. I must. . . ." Games. The games she and Cathy had played. They made resisting a demand come naturally —especially as Lottie's smiling, dimpled face appeared in the dark—a wall between herself and pleasure.

Jean Pierre's arms slackened. He held her from him. "I shall never take from you what you do not want to give," he said. Sarah sighed, relieved, disappointed. In anguish she moved from him. They gazed into the dark pond. What if he didn't hold her again? What if he didn't try? "But you wouldn't be sorry," he said. "I want to take you back with me."

"Take me back? You mean marry?"

"Africa will make you happy, Sarah," he said.

"I never thought of going to Africa." Her dreams had always taken her to Europe, home of great composers, or into America's jazz scene. Why not Africa, where, of course, jazz had had its genesis?

That reminded Sarah of Lottie not visiting Uncle Sam, and of Mrs. Johnson's reluctance to visit them. She shook the thoughts away. This seemed her night for insights that had to be thought out.

"What would your mother say?" Sarah asked. "She'd never accept anyone replacing her in your affections."

"No one ever shall."

"And your father?"

"What about him?" Jean Pierre countered. "What does he matter? He's old and against change. I believe only in change. I am still young.

"My father gave me all he had to give when he educated me. There's nothing more I want from him. He is not a good man—not decent. He has allowed the values of a beaten colonial power to rule his head. He loves me. I'm his only son. But he loves my mother and did not marry her because of the color of her skin. The one he married—she looks exactly like Madame Johnson. She has for him three daughters—but he only has love for me. His wife—they do not speak. She entertains his friends. And after an evening of *fête* he drives across the island to bed with my mother."

"And your mother allows it?"

"She adores him. Always. My mother—that beautiful woman—she has not married because of the love she have for this man. *Quelle misère.*"

"What does he look like?"

"Like me—a bit fairer—he is mulatto. His father, he was a Frenchman."

"And you want to marry me?" Sarah asked.

"I shall marry you, Sarah Richardson—or someone like you. I shall have a daughter with a round, dark face, round nose—*comme un bouton*—and bright intelligent eyes. She will know languages. I shall educate her. She shall play instruments."

"And know how to swim," Sarah said, laughing.

"Oh, yes, she shall know all things."

"What if you have a son?"

"It will be the same. I shall have many children and they shall all be talented. They must believe in work—with the hands. We in Africa must still work with yesterday's tools. And my children must know how to use the hands to reclaim deserts, keep water flowing, revitalize lands—forests —give to our land new life."

"How romantic you make it all sound. But I agree with Christophe, there's too much to do."

"Our—my life—the lifetime of generations." Dark, serious, his eyes gazed into hers. "This, my dear Sarah—I ask you to share."

The moonlit ground, the dark magic pond, the animals, the insects, the sleeping birds in the surrounding trees, all of it seemed so new, so new and wonderful. Sarah giggled. How stupid to giggle. She giggled again—sounding to all the world like a childish person bordering on insanity.

"Jean Pierre, I'm only seventeen," she whispered. "I'm too young to marry."

"In Africa girls marry when they can have children," he said.

"Here, we marry for love."

"You can have children, *n'est-ce pas?*"

"I'm only seventeen," she repeated, remembering that her mother had had her at sixteen—in another time.

"You have never seen the *sang?*" He frowned. Sarah blushed.

"Yes—I have my periods," she whispered.

"So—*quel problème?*"

"We've . . . just met," Sarah said, and wondered why

she kept saying stupid things. He had taken over her thoughts.

"That is not a problem," he said. "Do we need weeks, months, to know we go well together? Ah, lovely Sarah, talented Sarah, good, warm Sarah—of what are you afraid?"

A hundred things crowded her mind—above all Lottie's dark face, its angry eyes, its lovely dimples and perfect teeth. "I—I must finish school," she said. "By the time you come back to the States . . ."

"Sarah"—he moved from her—"I am not so young. Twenty-nine. I shall soon be thirty. I want children. I shall have them. And you? Do you always want to be waiting— outside of happiness? In this hemisphere—that's all that is promised."

He waited for her answer. What could she say? She wanted happiness, wanted him—his good looks, his charm, his intelligence. Why let him go? Why think of Lottie? In anguish she thought: *But I know nothing of forestry, or agronomy. . . .*

"Jean Pierre, please—kiss me again. . . ."

Twelve

The aroma of brewing coffee awakened Sarah the next morning. She lay staring at the ceiling, surprised that she had fallen asleep. Excitement had kept her awake most of the night. She had drifted in and out of sleep until deciding to remain awake and think things out. Dreams, a kaleidoscope of dreams, had paraded through the dark. At one moment she imagined herself at home playing the piano; at another moment, basket in hand, she floated over wide tracts of land, sprinkling handfuls of seeds into the earth, and watched as they pushed up green over the countryside.

At all times, in the background, Jean Pierre hovered, the most important presence in her life.

Uncle Sam? Lottie? They hadn't been in her dreams. They didn't know of her plans. Plans? To marry? She smiled. The room brightened with the rays of the rising sun. Then Sarah thought of Cathy.

The race? Had they made plans for the race? Getting out of bed, Sarah dressed and went downstairs, following the aroma of coffee into the kitchen, where Madame Armand was drinking her first cup of the morning.

"Where is everyone?" Sarah asked. "Aren't we going sailing?"

"Hummm, this coffee," Madame Armand responded, closing her eyes. "*C'est magnifique.* I make it myself."

"What about the race?" Sarah asked.

"You want that I pour you a cup?" Madame Armand said, pouring Sarah a cup without waiting for her to reply.

"What about the race?" Sarah said, taking the coffee.

"Race? Ha. The young ones. They are fast asleep. Jean Pierre? He is gone."

"Gone?"

"*Oui.* They telephone him last night. This morning he's gone. *Une crise de conscience.* He wanted to stay and see you. He couldn't wait." Sarah sat across the table from the woman. A crisis of conscience? While she lay in bed, dreaming, thinking silly thoughts, he had been down here, waiting to see her. She had been happy. Too happy? That sort of happiness belonged only in dreams.

"He's not coming back," she said.

"But of course, he must come back. Do you think he will leave his mama here? He borrow Clarice's car—and she must leave tomorrow, *n'est-ce pas?*"

"Will he have time to do all that he must and make it back for tomorrow?"

Madame Armand shrugged. "My son—he will do what he must."

"Then off to Africa?" Sarah said.

"That is his life. He choose it that way."

Sarah searched through the lovely brown eyes and saw the furtive loneliness lurking beneath their surface. She looked at the heavy golden wedding band on her finger. Madame Armand, seeing her looking at the ring, explained, "Jean Pierre, his father give this ring to me, to hold me to him. But it isn't the wedding band that hold me." They looked deeply into each other's eyes and looked away.

"Is Mama Dear sleeping too?" Sarah asked.

"Chère Mama, does she ever sleep? She's outside in her garden. Clarice, she is packing. She, too, is sad that she cannot go sailing."

"She can extend her time," Sarah said.

"My poor Clarice, she must work," Madame Armand said. "She has much to pay—her growing daughter, Mama Dear, that apartment in the city. Your country *est très difficile, n'est-ce pas?* Everything here is money."

Once again Sarah looked at the wedding band and noticed how soft her hands were—how long and smooth their fingers. They were different from Lottie's or Mrs. Johnson's hands. Everything about Madame spoke of luxury, a different style of life. "How long will you be staying?" she asked.

"Until Jean Pierre comes."

"Will he be leaving right away?"

"If his business is finished. He will go back only when all is done. Today he is in communication with a firm—*comment s'appelle . . .*"

"Farm?" Sarah asked. Madame Armand nodded.

"He is having trees shipped, hundreds of them—tons of seeds." She gazed into Sarah's eyes, expecting sympathy. Sarah looked back in amazement.

"My son, he is mad! Why is anyone importing trees and seeds to Africa? *Oui,* he is mad! Africa has jungles, forests, nothing but trees." Again she searched through Sarah's eyes for confirmation.

"He knows his work," Sarah said.

"He can stay at home and not have to work. His father, he is rich. There is work for him at home."

"His work is greater than you know," Sarah said. "It has to do with more than a little island, it has to do—with the world."

"Oh la la, but she defends him. My son has picked a good match." She smiled, to assure Sarah she had not been offended. "Well"—she shrugged—"Jean Pierre, he will take me home, then he shall go to quarrel with his father, then leave. I shall not see him again for many years."

"And you won't go with him," Sarah said.

"No, Jean Pierre, he is my son, not my lover. His father is my love—my lover."

"Are you happy?"

"What is happiness?" Madame Armand put her head back and played for a moment with her round, unlined neck. "Who is happy?" she asked.

"Wouldn't you be, if Jean Pierre's father was your husband?" Sarah asked, shocked at her boldness.

"He is my husband. He himself put this ring on my finger," Madame Armand answered. "I am his—his favorite concubine. We love each other—have since I was a young girl—twelve, thirteen. Jean Pierre cannot have everything. He cannot hate his country because it's too colonial, then respect the marriage vow only in front of a priest, *n'est-ce pas*?

"You see, when Jean Pierre's father, my lover, he tell me he cannot marry me, I didn't want no longer to live—not on that island. I wanted to die. But in this house—me, Mama Dear, Big Red, the children, the Dixons, what a big wonderful family."

"Then why did you go back to him?" Sarah asked.

"Because this country is not for me. Here I see no tenderness in the eyes of its men. Passion, *oui*. Tenderness, *non*. Men here desire. They want to possess—they do not know to love. And I—I must have tenderness—so much tenderness." Madame Armand pushed back her head, exposing a long, smooth neck. Her bare shoulders shone over a robe that had slipped to her breasts. She pulled her full breasts together, caressing them, and closed her eyes. "I must always have someone to love me, to touch me, to breathe life into me—tenderness. I think I want it so much because I am *orpheline*?"

"Orphan."

"Yes."

Sarah's eyes moved from the woman's neck to the shining shoulders, to her breasts. She stilled the urge to fall on her knees, to kiss the tiny feet in their dainty mules, to bury her face in the fullness of her breasts, mingle with her softness.

Hot tears burned the lids of Sarah's eyes. She stood up

abruptly and, leaving the sensuous woman to her thoughts, went outside. Avoiding the gardens, she took the path leading to the woods, where once more she plunged into its darkness.

She dawdled on the path, listening to scurrying animals and buzzing insects. It suited her mood. The night before had been rare, precious. Every nerve of her body tingled still from their closeness. During sleep she had decided to marry. She felt deeply the darkness that would fall in the lives of those she loved because of her decision. But she loved Jean Pierre more. His need for her was a new beginning that eclipsed everything. Her insistence on coming to the Cape, despite Cathy's rejection, she saw now as the hand of fate.

Sarah's feet sank into leaves cushioned by the slime of the plants rotting beneath. Gnats pestered her ankles. She fought through the twisted branches slowly, afraid to break through the clearing, afraid that the episode in the moonlight might have been a dream that the clear light of the day had washed away.

The image of the woman whom she had left alone in the kitchen came to mind. She thought of Lottie, and Mrs. Johnson, and shook her head. She wanted to be a Madame Armand. She wanted to marry Jean Pierre, to have him with her. She, too, needed so much tenderness.

Sarah came into the clearing, then wanted to reenter the gloom. But the running water drew her and she walked on in the direction of the pond. This, too, she reached quickly. Everything that had taken so much time in the moonlight took a few moments in the day. The daylight mocked her.

After thinking of Jean Pierre all night, of her response to him, it had been a shock to find him gone in the morning. With regret she thought of her having denied herself to him, of refusing what he had to give. Why? Because she was Lottie's child and had somehow decided that nothing she wanted in this life would come easy?

Picking up a pebble, Sarah threw it into the pond. The pebble sank without a ripple.

"You know what that pebble just tole me?" asked a voice, breaking the silence. Looking up, Sarah saw Mama Dear sitting on a large rock on the opposite bank.

"It didn't ripple," she said, surprised.

"It's the way you thrown it," Mama Dear said. Sitting on the rock, facing the rising sun, Mama Dear's face glowed with a strange radiance. Her skin from the distance appeared as satin; the white hair framed her face like a halo. It was strange to see her sitting there. Sarah thought she had seen her in the garden.

"What did the pebble tell you?" she asked.

"Tells me that you ain't been listening good to what I tells you."

"But I do," Sarah protested. "You said that if I wish and throw a pebble in the pond, the pond will ripple and—"

"And so it will." Mama Dear nodded. "But you must wish hard to make it come true, not just sit there staring."

So Sarah picked up another pebble and threw it. This one also sank without a ripple.

"Yes," Mama Dear said. "You're real scared to face life, honey. Ain't no way to be. If you 'fraid, that makes you go through life making all the wrong decisions—and always

145

having to be sorry after. Life's here, honey. You living it. Go on and wish on it."

Once again Sarah threw a pebble and watched as it sank.

"Look at me," Mama Dear said as she picked up a pebble and threw it almost to the center of the pond. That created a ripple, a ripple within a ripple, spreading out until it touched the surrounding land.

Sarah gazed with mounting respect at the woman enshrined by the sun. "See," she said. "You can't be scared to dream and hope and wish—especially when you're young and so talented. Believe me, if that water ripples, you will have the power to make that wish come true."

Sarah picked up another pebble, she held it in her hand, and closed her eyes to wish, then she threw it hard. It landed in the center of the pond. After a second, the water rippled, rippled, rippled. She laughed. She had wished that Jean Pierre, thinking of last night, would forget about his work and, turning around, rush back to her. And that was a silly wish.

Thirteen

 After leaving the woods Sarah collected her things from the house to go directly to the beach. She walked the two-mile stretch, at peace with herself for the first time since she had come. Alone, yet not lonely. She no longer needed Cathy, no longer had to cling to the fringe of Cathy's group.

She walked past the area that they had staked out as "their space," walking to the farthest end of the beach. On her way she stopped at a shop to rent a beach umbrella.

On her way out she had to wait for a small blond boy blocking the doorway—his arms so filled with swimming paraphernalia that he fumbled to open the door, dropping first his snorkels, then his goggles.

"Here, let me help," Sarah offered. She picked up his snorkels and goggles and relieved him of his flippers, leaving him holding only his rubber raft. "Looks as though you came to spend the day," Sarah said. She opened the door and they left the shop together.

"I'm here every day," he said. "Me and my mom. She's down to the beach already—sunbathing. I live in the water. You, you going in?"

"No," Sarah said, "I don't swim."

"Don't or can't?" the boy asked.

"Don't and can't," Sarah said. "I sit on the beach and read."

"My mother swims, but she don't. She just lies around—sunbathing. Hey, my name's Bobbie."

"Mine's Sarah. It's great to know how to swim," she said. "I have a friend who promised to teach me."

"Why don't you get yourself a raft like this one?" Bobbie said. "I'll teach you. All you got to do is lie on it and kick off. The water'll keep you afloat. Then you kick your feet and move your arms—I'll show you."

"Will you?" Sarah asked, then put down her umbrella and Bobbie's things, and ran back to the shop. After renting a raft she rejoined him and together they went to find his mother.

Bobbie's mother, a plump dark-haired woman with sunglasses, was already brown. Nevertheless, she lay stretched out on a blanket, fully exposed to the sun.

"You mind if I stay near?" Sarah asked. "Your son promised to teach me to swim."

"Help yourself," the woman answered. "It's not my beach. Anyway, I'm glad Bobbie's got somebody to play with—keeps him off me."

Bobbie took his things down to the water while Sarah

spread out her towel, a short distance away from his mother. She put up the umbrella and, lying down, opened *The Bluest Eye,* determined to finish the book. She had just begun when Bobbie came back.

"Sarah, the water's great. Come on."

"Let me finish this book first," Sarah answered. "I only have a few more pages."

"You can read it on the raft," Bobbie insisted. "Come on, I'll show you how."

Looking out over the water, she saw someone on a raft reading. So she took her raft and book and followed.

Standing at the water's edge, Bobbie said, "See, this is all you have to do." He pushed off on his raft, came back, pushed off again, came back again. Giving the book to Bobbie, Sarah bravely threw herself on the raft and pushed, then thrilled to the sensation of the raft floating away.

"Okay," Bobbie shouted—Bobbie always shouted. "Now do your arms like this—cup your hands, see." He floated alongside. In seconds he had left her far behind, then he came back. "See if you can do it," he commanded.

She did. Floating, lying on the raft. "Kick, kick," Bobbie shouted. She kicked, moved her hands, floated, out, out, out, with amazing ease. In seconds Sarah had put a great distance between herself and those floating at the water's edge. People wading near the shore already looked like sticks. Their cries were indistinct. A swimmer passed by. He didn't look at her as though he thought it strange that she, Sarah Richardson, was floating with nothing beneath her except a rubber raft. That put her at ease.

Bobbie gave her the book then and she observed, "Bobbie, there don't seem to be many people coming out this far."

"That's because the water's so deep," he said. Sarah grew still, still. She grew aware of being pulled and pushed by the ingoing tide. She opened her book, holding it high over her head to escape the occasional splashes of water.

Instead of reading Sarah found herself thinking of her uncle Sam and of her mother. Strange to have come to such an important decision concerning her future, without consulting either of them. When she had said yes to Mrs. Johnson, she had had no idea that her life might change—completely.

The wonder of it. Floating on the sea, she unlocked her mind from a lifetime of imprisonment. She liked the feel of it, this being in full control of the levers of her life. Free. Drifting away on her own.

Lottie's anger when she told her had to change to joy when she realized that she no longer had a daughter to worry about. No more buying clothes, books, music, or depending on her sister and brother-in-law. No more Thursday-night dinners.

Sarah laughed from pure happiness, just as the raft rode a giant wave, then settled down on the water with a thud. Sprays of water rushed over her, wetting her book.

"Boy, wasn't that great," Bobbie shouted. "Hey, hold this. I'm going in." He pushed his raft for her to hold, then dived into the water, disappearing beneath its surface.

Sarah held on to his raft, looking at her wet book, chagrined. Now she had to get to shore to dry it in the sun. She waited for Bobbie to surface. He didn't. She looked over the water. He was nowhere around. She looked for someone to tell. No one was near. She looked out at the distant beach, her fear of water rushing back. How to get back to the beach—to Bobbie's mother?

She tried to remember Bobbie's instructions—how to move her arms and legs, how to move the raft. Fear held her. She wanted to shout but saw no one to shout to. Then she looked down and saw Bobbie swimming beneath the water, beneath her raft. He came up beside her. "Why did you do that?" she cried in terror.

"What?" he asked. "That was great fun," he shouted. And Sarah, relieved, understood that anything that required effort along with danger had to be great fun to Bobbie.

Holding on to his raft, Bobbie tried to remount, but he slipped back into the water. He tried again and slipped back again. Finally, he shouted, "Hold it. Hold it." She held on, then he managed to remount. "What fun," he shouted. Sarah stared at him. What a fool to have followed him out into deep water. As much of a fool to have thought that she controlled the lever of her life.

She heard their shouts and looked toward the beach. She saw them running along the shore. The tide had carried her closer to "their space." She turned the raft around, and using her arms and legs, she tried to put distance between herself and them. She didn't want to be in the water with them.

Then she heard louder shouts. They had spotted her. Easy enough. She was the only black person in the water. Sarah kept moving but found herself pulling against the tide. She looked around for Bobbie. Their rafts had drifted apart. She saw his—nearer to the shore, where once again he attempted to remount.

Sarah looked again toward the beach. In relief she found they were gone. But relief changed when she saw swimmers heading toward her. Strong swimmers all, moving toward her. It had to be them—Cathy and her gang. But why did they want to swim toward her? Then she felt relief once again. They were no longer in the water. She looked around for the swimmers she had seen. How stupid. She relaxed, letting her raft drift. In her moment of panic the book had become completely wet.

She shook her head, annoyed with herself for having brought the book with her, annoyed about her fears. Why did she think she had anything to fear from them?

Then they were there, surrounding her—laughing, pulling and pushing at the raft. "Stop!" Sarah cried. "What are you doing? What do you want?"

"We heard you didn't know how to swim," Betty called. "So we came out to teach you!"

"I don't need you to teach me," Sarah cried.

"Don't look so scared," Jody said, laughing. "All you have to do is jump in. I'll hold you." That sounded reasonable and she thought of heeding him. But Milt and Cathy had come up on opposite sides of the raft, and started tilting it from one side to the other, preventing her from jumping in, even if she wanted to. She kept slipping and sliding, trying to grab first one side, then the next.

"Stop it. Do you hear me? I said stop it!"

"You stop being silly," Sarah heard Sheila's voice saying.

"When you hit the water, do the dog paddle. You won't drown."

"Yeah, all you have to fear is fear—that sort of thing, don't you know," Jody shouted, still laughing.

Of course. That was true. *Don't be afraid. Don't panic.* Sarah looked around in a panic—searching for Fred. She saw him treading water a distance from them. "Fred," she shouted to him, "I can't swim. You know I can't swim." He looked at her, then away, and called out to Cathy.

"Come on, Cathy, I'll race you back."

Cathy pretended not to hear. She held on to the raft. "You wanted a vacation, didn't you?" she hissed. "Well, here's your vacation. Enjoy."

They heaved, Cathy and Milt. The raft overturned. Sarah sank beneath the water. Holding her breath, moving hands, legs. Holding her breath. *Don't breathe, don't panic. Fear is all to be feared.* Holding her breath. Fighting against panic. *Think. Think.* Moving hands, legs, away from them—they moving from her. Holding her breath in, in—working legs. A bicycle. She worked her hands, held her breath. How long could one hold one's breath? Going to one side. Into someone. Moving away—into another body. Holding breath. *Think! Think! No panic!* Moving up, up. A touch on her head. Moving away from the touch. Up. Up. A hand on head! Holding her head! Forcing her down! Down. Down. Desperate. *Hold your breath. Tear at that hand. Rip that hand away. Fight that hand. Dig fingernails, deep, deep. Get free of that hand. Hold your breath. Fight that hand. Fight. Fight.* Fight a tearing in her chest. Sarah opened her mouth to scream.

The curtain of darkness moved back. Consciousness

flickered. She opened her eyes. Harsh lights blinded—blinding lights. The curtain closed. A roughness beneath her face. A rush of water, through her chest, her throat, her nostrils. Rough hands turned her. Rough hands on her face—a softness, pressing against her mouth, breathing her mouth, air filling her mouth, her lungs. . . .

Again the softness, lips pressed on lips, breathing, breathing, breathing. The shifting curtain, shifting, shifting, and again the hand holding open her mouth, a mouth. Wonderful lips. She opened her eyes. Sun glared back. She closed them. Tired. Tired. She had fought so hard, so hard. She closed her eyes, allowed the dark curtain to once again cover her mind.

Voices. Voices. Sarah opened her eyes and looked into the eyes of Prudence Dixon. She tried to sit up. A roaring—waves beating against her brains, forced her to lie still—still. She closed her eyes.

"Vous êtes des imbéciles! Criminals! *Oui!* Cursed children! Sick! Children of diseased souls!"

Sarah recognized the anger, then the voice. Jean Pierre. Jean Pierre? She turned her head to look at the door. Was Jean Pierre standing guardian outside her door? She looked around the brown-and-tan room, back into the eyes of Prudence Dixon.

"How dare you speak to me, to my friends, like that! How dare you accuse us? We were only playing."

"It's so you play? Pitching she who cannot swim into the sea?"

"Go-go-god-goddamn fo-fo-fo-for-foreigners." Milt? Lisping? Stammering? "Wh-wh-what d-d-d-do y-y-you kn-kno-know a-a-ab-about an-an-anything?"

"Mais ils sont des cannibals," from Madame Armand. "Never in my life I did see this—children killing children."

Betty (crying): "We're not murderers—we're not!"

Outside the door, crying, arguing. An inquest? Had she died? Once again Sarah struggled to sit up, only to be forced back by the roaring water in her head.

Jody McCoy: "We went to help her swim. She didn't want to. We were only having fun."

Mrs. Johnson: "Fun! You call that fun! Pushing a child's head under water?"

The hand over her head pushing her down, down, down. She had died! The hand, bursting her head, her chest, stretching, stretching.

Sarah opened her eyes. Stretching them wide, she moved them to see around the room—the desk, the bookcase, the portrait—the woman—Prudence—Prudence looked at her and winked. Welcoming her? Sarah stared, the woman smiled. Sarah closed her eyes. She didn't want to be dead. Didn't want to stay dead. Anxiously, she listened, wanting to hear voices at her inquest.

And she heard the voice of little Bobbie, from downstairs. He shouted, as he always did, "I seen him. I seen him. He and that girl. They pushed the raft over. And this guy—up there—that white one—he held her down."

Mama Dear (from the distance): "You must be sure, Bobbie. Honey, what you're saying is mighty serious—mighty serious indeed."

Bobbie (shouting): "But I did see him. The others, they

swam away. But this guy stayed behind holding her down. I got so scared. I got out of the water and went to get my mother."

Milt (shouting back): "Wh-wh-what y-y-you trying to pu-pu-pull, y-y-y-you li'l wh-wh-white ba-ba-ba-bast-bas-tard?"

Bobbie (screaming): "I seen you. I did. I did."

Sarah tightened the lids over her eyes, refusing to let them open to look at the smiling, winking Prudence. A deep well of loneliness was inside her. She cried, "Uncle Sam . . . Uncle Sam. . . ."

The door opened. "She said something. I heard her. I heard her." Mrs. Johnson. Sarah clutched the cover over her naked body, as she sensed the woman bending over her. "Sarah, speak to me. Say something. Tell me you're all right. If anything happened to you, Lottie will kill me."

Sarah opened her eyes and looked down at the head of the woman kneeling beside the bed sobbing. Mrs. Johnson looked up. Their eyes met and she cried, "Thank God. Thank God. Thank God. Thank Him for so many things. Thank Him for sending Jean Pierre back when he did so that he came in time to save you. Lottie would never have forgiven me. I wouldn't have forgiven myself if I had to be the cause of her suffering." But it was she who had wished Jean Pierre back. She who had tossed the pebble in the pond. Sarah lay still. She hated the woman's agony. She hated the sounds of her sobs—this woman who had allowed an apartment to come between her and her best friend. Now she wanted to bear the burden of her daughter's death. She hated the woman's agony, for it had nothing to do with her. It was the weight of Clarice Johnson's guilt. With sudden clarity Sarah saw the issues now had been joined.

Did she have to bear that burden too? Had she almost died for something so ordinary in the lives of plain, hard-working people? Something so ordinary, that seemed so extraordinary to them.

Sarah looked up from the woman's bowed head and across the room into the eyes of her daughter. Cathy had come into the room and now stood with her back guarding the closed door. Their eyes met—and spoke, Sarah's saying, *So, Cathy, you wanted me dead.* And the smoky blue eyes narrow with hatred responding with vindictiveness, *I see you didn't die—yet.* Sarah shivered.

$\mathcal{F}$ourteen

 Something, someone, had awakened her. . . . Sarah opened her eyes. She stared into the surrounding darkness, listening. Her body burned, yet she shivered. Her teeth chattered. Death seemed to stand near. Her eyes tried to pierce through the darkness. She had learned death. It always stood near—beneath the surface of sullen faces, woven into mocking smiles, tooled into smoky, hate-filled eyes. It had come to try again. . . .

Sarah strained, trying to hear movement in the dark room. As she listened, she experienced again the feeling of having been capsized in the water. She tasted the salt. She felt herself sinking. Down, down, down. Then in a flash, she had conquered fear. In that instant she had moved hands and feet, propelling herself upward to the surface. Elation. She had saved herself! Then the hand—that hand on her head, pushing her, pushing down, down to her death.

Sarah shivered. Shivered. Someone stood in that room. She wanted to call Cathy by name, demand what she wanted. Instead she found her body curling into a shivering ball.

"Chérie, pourquoi tu trembles? I am here."

Jean Pierre, standing by the bed, guarding her? Relieved. Happy. Nevertheless, her teeth chattered. *"Non, chérie.* You must not be so cold." He left. Sarah shivered. Not from fear. She had him with her, in the house. She had nothing to fear.

Between fits of sleep and awareness she felt him near again. The light came on. He knelt beside the bed forcing something—brandy—down past her chattering teeth. She tried to sip. She coughed. The burning liquid cut off her air. She coughed, coughed, kept coughing. He took her into his arms then, bent her back, then he slipped in beside her. Taking his robe, he wrapped it around her, pulling her so that they lay skin touching skin. He pulled her close, close. The heat of his body passed slowly through her; first her teeth stopped chattering, then the muscles of her neck loosened, then the muscles of her back. Then her shivering ceased.

With warmth came sleep. She fought against sleep. She was afraid that if she slept he might leave again, go away, leaving her alone, and as lonely as she had been earlier.

In desperation she folded her arms around him, holding him to her. She slept and felt him move. She awakened and held him closer still. She moved into him, moved into him, her fears of the night yielding to a new demand. He must not leave her. She would not let him leave her weak, vulnerable, a child still. She needed him, his strength, to make her strong again. She held him to her, demanding that he respond to her fevered passion. And his penis, hard against her leg, hardened more. He pulled her beneath him, entered her. She groaned. Pushed up into pain. He pushed down, down, and she held his hot body to her, in her, blending their heat, blending their heat, blending their heat . . .

A roaring in her head, their burning, twisting bodies cemented, carried her into madness. They came as one. He held her, held her, whispered—*"Mon amour, mon amour, mon amour"*—then, *"Voilà, mon amour,* you are no longer so young." They fell asleep together, wrapped around each other.

When she awoke, Jean Pierre was gone.

Sarah lay watching the room brighten. Moving her hands around areas of pain, of pleasure. Already she missed the touch of Jean Pierre's hot flesh, the smoothness of his body. Her throat was still sore from vomiting. But her body felt pleasantly languid. She kept waiting, hoping that he might come again, to make love to her again, accustom her to this new delightful sensation that she had willed to herself— forever.

The door opened, and hearing Mrs. Johnson's voice, she closed her eyes, "Jean Pierre is already gone," Mrs. Johnson said. "I don't think I can go, too, not until I know that Sarah's fully recovered." Disappointment, so deep, so deep, made a dryness in her mouth. He had gone. She hadn't been able to hold him.

"*Mais,* Clarice, your work," Madame Armand reminded her. "I am here."

"I would have felt so much better if she had had a doctor," Mrs. Johnson said.

"Jean Pierre, he say there's no need. If he say so, it is so. I am here, Clarice. I shall take good care of our Sarah. I shall make her good, strong tea of mint with rum and honey. She will be—how you say—born again."

"Sure, Clarice." Mama Dear's voice. "Sarah'll be all right. No need to worry. Nobody dies from drowning—after they been saved."

Disappointment had forced her to keep her eyes closed. But as she felt them moving away, she opened her eyes, and seeing them leaving she wanted to shout: *Don't go. I'm sick. I want to be sick. I almost died! I need attention. I need Mrs. Johnson's agony, Madame's tea with mint, rum, and honey. Don't leave me.*

Her panic lasted a second, then she heard Mama Dear. "Nobody dies from drowning—after they been saved. . . ."

And indeed a new vitality filled her. She jumped up from bed. Too quickly. Dizziness forced her to sit, then to lie back down. She moved to cover herself and noticed the sheet on which she lay, stained with blood. So much blood? What should she do? If Mama Dear came and tried to straighten the sheet!

Sarah closed her eyes. Later. She would decide what to do later. Curving her body around the bloody stain, she fell asleep.

Sarah awakened in early afternoon, surprised that she felt

no real effects of her near drowning. She got out of bed, pulled off the bloodstained sheet and the mattress cover, which was also bloodstained, took them into the bathroom, and washed the stains off. Then she took them out on the terrace and spread them out over the rail. A confession to those who chanced to look up—and ask.

Sarah laughed as she left the room. Never had she felt so warm, so tender—a wonderful tenderness. She heard voices from the parlor as she went down the stairs, and when she came to the landing, suitcases stood at the foot of the stairs. Were they all leaving?

"I tell you, when li'l Bobbie tole me what happen"— Mama Dear's voice—"I liked to gone clean out of my head. I was that near calling the police. Thank God, Jean Pierre and Clarice stop me. That's never been the way we settle things around here. Big Red never did have no truck with the police. And the Dixons would not have heard of it."

"I—I—I ke-ke-keep te-te-tel-telling y-y-y-you the li-li-li'l br-br-bra-brat li-li-lied." Milt stood in the middle of the parlor, his face twitching. All eyes were on his spindly body, loony look, watching his rapid disintegration. "Th-th-those wh-w-white bas-bas-bastards li-li-lie a-a-about ev-ev-every-everything."

"I don't understand," Mama Dear insisted. "How y'all say you was playing with Sarah in that deep water when y'all hardly want to talk to her on dry land?"

"Ho-ho-how we know Sa-Sa-Sarah co-co-cou-coul-couldn't sw-sw-swim? Sh-she's ou-ou-out th-th-there o-on the be-be-beach ev-ev-every day i-in th-th-that bi-bi-bik-bikini."

"*Mais oui,* but you know," Madame cried. "The other day when me and Clarice come from the boat and see you on the beach, we tell you we leave Sarah with Jean Pierre. We say to you she stay because she cannot swim."

"W-w-we g-g-got th-th-the i-id-idea she st-stayed for oth-other reasons." Despite his stuttering Milt tried a leer. "As-as-ask th-them." He looked around at those sitting around, staring at him with disbelieving eyes. "Di-di-didn't w-we?"

Eyes turned to Sarah at the door, then turned away.

"How dare you?" Mrs. Johnson stood up to confront him, silencing him. "How dare you all"—she looked at them heaped together on the couch—"blame your criminal actions—yes, I said criminal—on such base assumptions!"

"Clarice, don't upset yourself," Mama Dear said. "It's all over now. I called them numbers you give me and I told their folks to be expecting them—I told them exactly what happened."

"What?" Cathy jumped to her feet and rushed to stand over the old lady. "Who do you think you are, asking my friends to leave, then calling their parents without telling me?"

Mama Dear rocked in her squeaking chair. Her face had become still. "Yes, I told 'em to pack up, and I told their folks to expect them. Their folks had to know that their children was leaving my house safe. No one leaves this house dead if they ain't in the family."

"If anyone ought to leave, let it be Sarah. I didn't invite her. Mother did!"

The slap resounded throughout the room. Mama Dear

stood up, but it took seconds for all to realize that Mama Dear had slapped her enraged granddaughter. Then Mrs. Johnson rushed to Mama Dear's side and the two women faced Cathy. The rocking chair kept rocking, squeaking, underlining the thundering silence in the room.

Cathy worked her hands into fists. Sarah kept wondering, *Would she dare? Will she dare?* But she kept them at her sides.

"Cathy Johnson," Mama Dear said when she had regained her calm, "I dare anything I must. And I figured I must invite your friends to leave this house—and ask them never to come again."

"This is my father's house," Cathy shouted, pushing her face down to her grandmother's. "It's my home, left to my father by his father. That's why my mother works to help maintain it. For us!"

"If that's the tale you been telling, li'l girl, it's a mighty sorry tale. This house belongs to folks of good thoughts and deeds. Big Red and me worked hard to keep it that way. Never before has anyone brought murder right to this door. And you say to me you got the right?"

"This is too awful," Sheila cried, jumping to her feet. She came to stand beside Cathy. "Please, Grandmother, please, believe me. I meant Sarah no harm. I did swim out with the others. We were teasing. I know we haven't been nice to Sarah since we came. I wasn't nice—always belittling her. I never gave a thought to what my actions might lead to. I can't stand the idea, that you—that she"—she turned to look at Sarah, her eyes, wide, frightened—"that anyone can think I wanted to kill . . . Sarah, forgive me." Tall, thin, she now appeared younger than her eighteen years. Sarah knew that Sheila might be the reason she was still alive. Sarah heard her still: "When you hit the water, do the dog-paddle." And she had. She had almost saved herself—until the hand . . .

Betty and Jody stood up too. "Mama Dear, I—I'm glad you didn't call the police," Betty said. She kept crying, sniffling. "I never meant to hurt anybody. I don't know what happened. That's the God's truth."

"That's true, Mrs. Johnson," Jody said. "We were just playing around. Like Milt said. Then Cathy saw Sarah. Cathy had been looking for her—I think. You had told us that Sarah had gone to the beach. I figured to get away from us, so I didn't see why we should be looking for her. We hadn't been exactly nice the night before.

"I didn't even want to see her. But Cathy kept searching, then she said, 'Isn't that Sarah out there on that raft?' Then Milt said, 'Dig that. I don't believe that girl. She's got to be kidding, do you see her in that white bikini?' Then Cathy said, 'What are we waiting for?' "

"Yes," Betty said. "Then we were all running. Something had happened to us—something weird. Like a mob. We took off screaming, loud, hysterical almost. Whatever it was, I didn't want to but I couldn't stop myself. I had to go along."

"There we were in the water," Jody took it up again. "Swimming, swimming. Somehow I knew it wasn't just fun and games anymore."

"No," Betty whispered. "It wasn't just fun and games. Yet we kept going along. I'm so ashamed."

165

"Yep." Jody stared out of the doorway, anxious to be gone. "That's the way it happened. I—I want to thank you and Jean Pierre—more than anyone Jean Pierre. It had to be a miracle him coming back when he did." He put his arm around Betty. They walked from the parlor. Sheila followed.

Fred, too, stood up and went toward the door. Madame Armand stopped him. "You, too, my beautiful one?"

Fred turned to face her in anguish. "Me more than most, Madame. I am guilty. I accept full blame for my actions, but I never thought it would come to this. I knew Cathy held a grudge against Sarah. Why? I don't know. Guys like Milt, I've been knowing all my life. Confused cats who got to hate for its own sake. He always took off on dark-skinned folks. The only way to keep them off you is to whip them. When I saw Sarah had come, I was relieved. I didn't have to keep beating on his butt to keep him off me.

"But it wasn't so much Milt as Cathy. She had it together all the way. She set the tone. And I knew what was being put down. I could have stopped it—but I guess I lacked something . . . courage."

"Integrity," Mrs. Johnson said.

Fred shrugged. "Whatever. I—I—everybody knows what I felt for Cathy. I was crazy about her and couldn't believe my luck when she fell for me. They—Cathy and the rest of their friends—they set boundaries that they don't let most folks get through. They let me. I wanted to keep it that way. So you see . . ." He looked around at them all. "But I had had it and was ready to pull out before this happened." He looked at Sarah. "Look, I'll see you in town. It's something we got to talk out."

Sarah understood Fred. She had always felt Cathy's pull and even now, with all that had happened, she felt a nostalgia for the excitement, the challenge—the times spent on the other side of their youth.

As Fred was speaking, Milt kept walking around the parlor like someone caged. His lips were white, as though drained of blood. "I—I—I don't gi-gi-gi-give a da-damn wh-wh-what th-th-they say. A bu-bu-bunch of cowards. Li-liars. P-pu-push a gu-guy in-into so-so-something, th-th-then go ba-ba-backing out."

Sarah felt a rush of pity for the gangling youth, who didn't seem to understand the full implications of his actions. He had gone far beyond his depth and might never be able to pull himself out. Cathy's victim. But Cathy had no pity.

"Cathy," Mrs. Johnson said, "do you think your friend can drive? Or is anyone going with him who can?"

"Sheila drives."

"Good. Then please see them to their cars."

They left, carrying their bags. The house took on the air of a fortress deserted after battle.

"Mother, I have tried so hard," Mrs. Johnson agonized. "I did everything I know how."

The old woman kept rocking, shaking her head. "It ain't your fault, Clarice. That child had to be a hard one to raise. She's her granddaddy's own mean child. Got all his fault and none of his goodness.

"I can see her now sitting astride her granddaddy's knee.

167

I hear him talking about men what he had killed, and men what his granddaddy killed. He'd tell her, 'My granddaddy was the power. I ain't about to be nobody's victim. Don't you never in life be nobody's victim. . . .' "

"She's got to change," Mrs. Johnson said. "What's to become of her?"

"She'll change when the world change," Mama Dear said. "Till this hemisphere learns to cure its disease. Cathy's infected—bad. It's the rest of us what got to worry. Wouldn't you say so, my li'l Sarah?" She smiled.

"After all my work," Mrs. Johnson protested. "I spent my life: Going back to school after college, training to be a decorator, even working at that civil service job, to keep her butt in Banning, to keep clothes on her back, while helping you out up here. Now you say there was nothing to be done from the first?"

"Everything you did went into making her special," Mama Dear said.

"Mrs. Johnson"—a piece of puzzle had been floating around Sarah's mind, since her argument with Cathy. She had to know—"did you ever tell my mother not to come to visit you?"

"Never!" Mrs. Johnson cried. "Where did you hear a thing like that? From your mother, most likely."

"No, not from my mother. Cathy told me that I ought to be more like my mother and stop going where I wasn't wanted."

Mrs. Johnson shook her head. "Never have, Sarah. There was one time when Lottie came to my job, I told her it was better if the boss didn't see her. I didn't want him to be asking those questions. You know—is she? Isn't she? I couldn't afford to lose my job. So I told Lottie to cool it, that I'd see her back at my apartment. Lottie didn't come. She never came after that. You know Lottie, how she's always taking things the wrong way."

"You told my mother not to come to your job." Sarah's heart constricted.

"Don't make it sound as though I committed a crime, Sarah," Mrs. Johnson said. "With all the hoopla of what a great city we live in, we all know that there are places blacks can't go. I wouldn't have been hired if my boss had known that I was black. And the Lord knows I worked and studied hard to earn the right to my profession. Still, I can't have my friends hanging around my job. Lottie knows these things. But instead of supporting me and being happy for me, she goes around condemning me!"

"She didn't," Sarah flared. "She never told anyone. She'd be too ashamed to tell that her best friend—" Suddenly Sarah understood: Shame. Lottie's shame expressed itself as rage!

The room stopped breathing. Eyes all turned to Clarice Johnson. "Hey, look here," she protested to break through their condemnation. "I'm a woman raising a child out here by herself. I got to work. Sure, I have a weakness. Ambition. But that weakness happens to be my strength. I made it to where I am today because of my ambition. Nobody gave me one thing. I worked hard for everything I got. So don't go trying to pin guilt trips on me!"

Time stretched, stretched, stretched. Sarah's pain grew

more unbearable. If she hadn't understood her mother, what did she understand in this entire world?

Mama Dear's eyes, when she looked at her daughter-in-law, were filled with pity. Caring was woven into the fine lines around them. "A mistake," she said, rocking to erase the numbing silence. "An unhappy mistake. Problem is, it ain't ours—never ours—to decide. Yet it's us what got to be responsible. Whatever happen, we got to keep loving one another. Got to examine things and talk them out—or these mistakes we making today spills over from one generation to the next—getting thicker and thicker with each new layer. . . ."

Upset by what sounded like an apology for Mrs. Johnson, and for Cathy, Sarah stared at the old woman. "But I nearly died," she whispered.

"But you didn't die," the old lady rebuked her. "Just like I didn't die in the old South and Big Red didn't die. We live long enough to see and appreciate that among the best folks bad things ferment, and among the worst folks good things flow. Them li'l ones," she said as they heard the dying sounds of the cars' motors, "they still children. They ain't about to get over what they done, Sarah. It's y'all's experience, and all of you got to learn, and be better people because of it." She chuckled. "Bet no one's more surprised than they seeing the evil they can do and how far they'd go in trying."

She kept rocking and sighing in the silent room. "Sarah, we all, in one way or another, are people we think we're not."

Fifteen

Sarah pushed through the curtain of branches into the clearing, then turned to look back into the woods. Memories of the first night, the moonlit night when she and Jean Pierre had fought their way through, haunted her. So much had happened since then. But now this too-short, too-tragic, wonderful, never-to-be-duplicated vacation was nearing its end. She and Madame Armand were Mama Dear's last remaining guests, since Cathy and her mother had gone two days before. Two days that Cathy and Mrs. Johnson had spent not looking at each other, hardly talking, as though they wanted to be free of the other's presence. The strain of the two days had told on all of them. Now there remained only herself and Madame Armand, waiting for the return of Jean Pierre.

Slowly, Sarah walked on toward the pond, measuring her

steps. Uncle Sam and Aunt Gladys were on their way—coming to take their Puddin' home. Only the name Puddin' no longer fit. It had been tattered to shreds in the upheaval of this summer. Strange, the rolling ball of circumstances that had begun to pull apart when she had defied Lottie and had decided to come. One of the casualties had definitely been the name Puddin'.

Sarah wondered what Lottie had said to Mrs. Johnson when she had gone to see her and had told her of her daughter's near-tragic end? Had Lottie reacted in horror, or with her I-told-you-so rage? Did it matter? As Mama Dear had said: "But you didn't die."

Reaching the pond, Sarah stood on its bank, brooding into the dark, still water. Then she picked up a pebble, made a wish, and threw it. The pebble skimmed the surface of the water to the center and sank. Sarah waited—seconds, minutes. The water had to ripple as it had when she had wished for Jean Pierre to be at her side in times of danger. It was that wish that had brought him back to save her life. She knew it. Finally the water rippled, and the ripples grew, spreading out, out, to wash the bank. Hurriedly she made another wish. She hadn't died. Nothing had ended. But despite, or perhaps because of, her near death, she had begun to see so much more clearly. Perhaps one might call it the start of wisdom.

"We all are people we think we're not." She heard Mama Dear's words loud, clear. She looked over at the rock on the opposite bank expecting to see Mama Dear, or some of those who haunted the old house. "We are all the people we think we're not." So many of the things she listened to when Mama Dear spoke, she only heard long after.

Those words made her think of Clarice Johnson and Lottie Richardson. Who did they think they were? Clarice Johnson was a good woman and by her standards fair minded. She had been well educated, coming from what is respected as a "good family." Mrs. Johnson had worked hard to achieve what she wanted in life. She knew she had limitations and she had accepted that. She had arrived.

Lottie Richardson believed herself to be a great woman. Black, plump, abandoned, with a limited education. She had had to fight for everything. She worked hard—with a passion. She did not accept any limitations. Limitations enraged her, kept her locked in a perpetual struggle that she saw as only a beginning. Whether she arrived or not was never a question—she had prepared herself to be a strong swimmer in this life.

Sarah and Cathy had always been a part of their parents' agenda. Lottie had preserved Sarah's innocence—insurance for her lifelong swim. Cathy had never been innocent. Her restless spirit, her negative forces, her strength might be curbed, but never changed. Big Red's rage drove her. Rage at his father, his grandfather. The rage that had bypassed his son to settle in Cathy. What was to become of Cathy? Despite near death at her hands Sarah felt an obligation to care.

Perhaps as Cathy grew old, lonely, and friendless, she might be able to see through the fog of her rage and to determine the enemy—and use her anger *for* friends instead of against them.

Picking up another pebble, Sarah threw it into the pond. This time as she waited for the water's ripple from behind her she heard, "Sa-rah . . ." Then the water did ripple and her body responded to the sound from behind her. His voice. Her heartbeat quickened, her breath came in gasps from a trembling body. "Sa-rah, *j'arrive*. Where are you?"

"*Ici,* Jean Pierre, I am here."

The woods came alive with the screeching of angry birds, animals scurrying, and the hitting together of the leafy branches. It remained so for seconds, then settled down into silence. Sarah waited for the branches to part. Was he really as handsome as she kept thinking him? Whatever, she loved him. Oh, how she loved him! The branches parted and there he stood, beautiful, this black man, in a white cotton suit. They stood staring at each other over the vast expanse. She held her breath, wanting him to speak, wanting him to be the one to tell how he had missed her. She wanted to know. How did she look to him now? Ordinary since their separation?

The restrained moment passed and they ran, pulled to each other, fell into each other in a sort of desperation, holding, holding, then they kissed.

"Jean Pierre, I—I am so glad. I thought I might never get the chance to see you again."

"*Comment?*" His surprise at her words, his confusion, touched her with sadness. "But how you think this thing? You are seeing me for always, *chérie.*"

"No . . ." The pain of it, the terrible brutal pain of it. "I —I'm leaving tomorrow. My aunt and uncle are coming to take me home—they'll be here this evening."

The light in his eyes died. A deep frown divided his brow. "But you cannot go home with them—not to stay," he said. "You must come with me. You promised."

Promised? Had she? Did it matter? Their being together, loving each other, had been the promise. The one that mattered. That he had come back to find her in this golden mist —that mattered.

"*Chérie,* you are not angry with me?" Jean Pierre searched through her eyes. "I did not want to leave you so soon. But Mama Dear, she was here. My mother, she was here. Mrs. Johnson too. I—I had to go. It is important that I had to."

"Your work went well?" she asked, not wanting him to take the blame for something for which he had no responsibility. "You succeeded with what you came here to do?"

"*Oui,* I did." Jean Pierre nodded. Immediately his black eyes shone again. "I sign many contracts. I go back to Africa to await the shipment of grains, tons of grains—trees."

"I'm so glad." Sarah smiled up at him.

"Me, too, I am glad. I love my work, Sarah."

Sarah moved her eyes over him, quickly, to keep every part of him in her mind, to lace him into her nightly dreams —his broad shoulders, the muscular arms, his black, beautiful face with its bright eyes—brilliant whites, the gems of blackness. Had there ever been another man like him—in the entire world? "You are the most perfect man." She hadn't known she was going to say that. He laughed uncomfortably.

"*Moi?* Me? I who have no time, never, to give the sweet nonsense women crave? I who must run around his whole life—a man possessed to right wrongs, which, of course, he cannot. No man such as this can ever be perfect, *mon amour.*"

Sarah reached up to touch his face. She kissed him. Kissed the mouth that had given her back her life. Her very life, for which, if for no other reason, she ought to follow him, go wherever he chose. Her tenderness, her gentle touch, forced his laughter. "I love you, Sarah Richardson. Do not tease me. You must come away with me to make this life possible for me to go on."

"Jean Pierre. I'm only seventeen."

"So?"

"I am too young to marry."

"But, *chérie,* you are no longer so young," he teased her, and Sarah blushed, remembering.

"Yes, I am no longer so young. And even here, Jean Pierre, girls marry young. I can't." She hadn't thought out what to say. Certainly she hadn't expected to plead a cause for their separation. She had decided to remain Lottie Richardson's little girl a bit longer. She thought that the sight of him had to wipe away that resolve.

It wasn't the life she wanted—hard work, constant practice, Thursday-evening dinners—all stretched out, a limitless bore without Cathy's devious presence.

"Chérie." Jean Pierre's confusion was reflected in his eyes. "You must not be serious—being with you is so important to me, my life."

"My uncle wants me to be a star," Sarah answered.

Shaking his head in disbelief, Jean Pierre stepped back from her. *"Mais—c'est pas possible.* You choose to throw me away to become a court jester?"

"Never!" She had expected pain, but not this hurting. "We Black American artists are not court jesters, Jean Pierre. We are the artistic vitality of this country. We are Africa in the United States—in the Americas—in this hemisphere."

"And you believe that you shall show this to the world by playing Chopin?"

"We put no limits to our talents, Jean Pierre. We absorb all that's out there to be absorbed—and create the new. It's only through the new that we survive."

"You believe you shall succeed?" he asked. Sarah nodded. "And that will make you happy?" She nodded again.

"I am very talented," she said.

"*Oui*—you are." Jean Pierre nodded too. "And so you owe me—our love—nothing?"

He had decided to let her go! Without a struggle! She didn't want him to let her go! "I owe you my life, Jean Pierre! My intelligence!"

True. Before him becoming famous had been the only way she could see to escape forever living on the fringes of doomed neighborhoods, fighting, always fighting, for every inch of space, to live, to work. Knowing him, loving him, had brought light into her life. He had opened up new horizons. He had given her choices.

"You opened up the world for me, Jean Pierre." She walked back into his arms, clung to him. "Jean Pierre, will you marry me?"

"What? But you just say . . ."

"That I want to marry you. That I shall marry you—but not now."

"*Chérie,* you are the dreamer."

"Jean Pierre, listen to me. It's you who say we must look at our history. I am looking at history—today's history.

"My uncle lives in the innermost part of the inner city. He stayed on there working when he might have done other things. He did it to give me a start in what he knew. Music. He bought me my first piano—a baby grand. Do you know how much that cost—a janitor?

"Most of those he knew moved away. Old friends died. Yet those for whom he sacrificed refused to visit him. They're afraid of his blighted neighborhood. One day—I see clearly—that old building falling in, burying him. If I cannot give back to him something for which he has paid so dearly, then what's the use . . . ?"

"And so you can disappoint me, Sarah, you who say you want to marry but can't? Our children—what about them?"

He spoke gently—with understanding. And because she felt his tenderness, what might have been simple heartbreak became the agonizing problem of her life.

"I didn't say I can't." She searched his face. "I'm saying I can't now. Jean Pierre, my mother has worked hard—so hard." Sarah hadn't meant to bring Lottie's name up. She hadn't thought of Lottie as part of the equation. But there she stood, squeezing in between them, her dimples digging into her pretty, dark face, her no-nonsense smile waiting to tighten in defeat.

"Yes, she worked hard. Yet never have I seen a man's arms around her—as yours are around me. Never have I seen tenderness in a man's eyes when he looked at her—as you are now looking at me." The need Madame Armand had talked about, Sarah knew, suddenly. And she knew that Lottie had missed out on it. "No one has ever thought to even buy her a gold band—to bind her with love. Never has she been supported by a mate. She's been alone—so alone, Jean Pierre."

Tears pushed out of Sarah's eyes. They rolled down her cheeks, tears as big as those she had shed on her way from the beach. So many tears she had never known she had to shed. Yet they stemmed from one source. The vacation, the time away, had brought them out, had forced the realization that she had always known her mother's deep enduring loneliness, her pain, without thinking it out.

Yes, she had condemned Lottie's rages and had never examined their cause.

"It's historical, Jean Pierre," Sarah repeated. "It's what we owe to each other."

Jean Pierre's arms tightened around her. "What to say?" he murmured. "But know the ways of the world, *ma petite.* Waiting I cannot promise. People meet, they love, they marry—or they don't. They live together or they live apart. They sometimes forget."

"I shall never," Sarah promised.

"Sarah, I want children." Jean Pierre smiled sadly. "I am not so young—almost thirty. . . ."

"You must wait until . . ."

"You become a star?" He wiped the tears from her cheeks with tender fingers. "Sarah, I shall always be happy to see you. Pleased when I hear of your success."

Sarah clung to him in desperation. "I love you. There's no one else in all the world for me. I have never seen you before, Jean Pierre Armand, not in films, nor have I read of you in books. I can't bear to lose you. Wait for me," she wailed. "I promise—"

Jean Pierre pulled her to his chest. "I promise that I shall write to you, Sarah Richardson. I promise you to let you know of my work and to always know of yours. You see, *chérie*, I, like your uncle Sam, have the confidence."

"And when I come to you, Jean Pierre, I swear to you that I shall know all there is to know"—Sarah saw herself strolling through Central Park, kicking the brown leaves swirling at her feet, looking up at trees stripped bare by cold winds, and talking about them to Lottie Thursday nights when she prepared dinner—"about forestry and agronomy, I swear . . ."

"Mais, vous êtes un poète, ma petite Sarah." Jean Pierre smiled at her, pushing his fingers through her thick hair.

"Yes, I am a poet," Sarah agreed. "What's more, I threw a pebble into the pond and the water, rippled, rippled, rippled. . . ."